DADDY FOR THE MIDWIFE'S DAUGHTER

SUE MACKAY

Recycling programs for this product may not exist in your area.

ISBN-13: 978-1-335-95288-2

Daddy for the Midwife's Daughter

For questions and comments about the quality of this book, please contact us at CustomerService@Harlequin.com.

Harlequin Enterprises ULC
22 Adelaide St. West, 41st Floor
Toronto, Ontario M5H 4E3, Canada
www.Harlequin.com

HarperCollins Publishers
Macken House, 39/40 Mayor Street Upper,
Dublin 1, D01 C9W8, Ireland
www.HarperCollins.com

Printed in U.S.A.

1 2 3 4 5 6 7 8 9 10 HDC 29 28 27 26

Then there was the signing of her contract followed by tapping of glasses and the first sip of bubbles and everyone saying, "Welcome aboard, Caia." She hadn't felt this good in a long time.

Then she glanced at Lockie and felt a hit of heat in her stomach. How did he do that? She wasn't interested in him. Just because he could wind her tighter than a ball of string didn't mean she intended getting to know him on a personal level. She didn't need another man letting her down.

Anyway, he'd said he led a very full life, so there'd be no spare time for someone else by the sound of it. That was something else she didn't want—a man who didn't have time for her and McKenzie. McKenzie was not growing up knowing what it was like to have her father figure walk away from her. Never. Caia would remain single until McKenzie was old enough to be setting up her own life as she chose.

Dear Reader,

During the worst day of her life, Caia bumped into a stranger and poured out her fears over her daughter's chances of survival. The next time she sees Lockie Johnstone, he's one of three GPs interviewing her for a midwife position at their practice. He's never forgotten the vulnerable woman he spoke to and has often wondered how everything turned out for her and her daughter.

Caia is taken on, and working in the same practice comes with some difficulties as they are continuously aware of each other. When Lockie asks her out, Caia instantly says no. She can't afford to fall out with him after a date and have to work alongside him.

Lockie needs to get Caia out of his system so he can get back to an even keel with his busy life. But what are the chances of that happening? Seems neither of them can let go of their pasts, but nor can they walk away from each other.

I hope you enjoy reading their story and seeing how they manage to overcome their trust issues.

All the best,

Sue MacKay

Sue MacKay lives with her husband in New Zealand's beautiful Marlborough Sounds, with the water on her doorstep and the birds and the trees at her back door. It is the perfect setting to indulge her passions of entertaining friends by cooking them sumptuous meals, drinking fabulous wine, going for hill walks or kayaking around the bay—and, of course, writing stories.

Books by Sue MacKay

Harlequin Medical Romance

Stranded with the Paramedic
Single Mom's New Year Wish
Brought Together by a Pup
Fake Fiancée to Forever?
Resisting the Pregnant Pediatrician
Marriage Reunion with the Island Doc
Paramedic's Fling to Forever
Healing the Single Dad Surgeon
Brooding Vet for the Wallflower
Wedding Date with the ER Doctor
Parisian Surgeon's Secret Child
A Fling with the ER Doc
Enemy on Her Hospital Ward

Visit the Author Profile page at Harlequin.com for more titles.

For my family and close friends. You are my stars.

CHAPTER ONE

'CAIA? I'M LOCKIE ROBERTS, one of the partners of North Shore Medical Centre. Come through and meet the rest of the crew.' He sucked in a lungful, unable to believe the apparition standing before him. 'This way.' Or better yet, the front door's over there.

'Pleased to meet you, Lockie.' There was no hitch in her voice. No heat creeping into her face, as he was certain was happening to his. Instead, she calmly held her hand out to him.

Reluctantly, he shook it. Equally reluctantly, he let go as more heat flared. She didn't recognise him. That had to be good. It had only been a fleeting connection when they'd locked eyes over a water cooler on a ward at Auckland Children's Hospital. Dressed in scrubs and wearing a mask, she was shaking so hard the water in her paper cup splashed everywhere. He'd refilled it for her, asking if she was all right.

Not really, she'd whispered, tugging her mask away. *My daughter's waiting for a stem cell trans-*

plant. She's got leukaemia. She hadn't cried, but the pain resonating in her voice had brought back memories of his family going through a similar experience when his brother had acute leukaemia. He'd said, *That's beyond difficult.*

She'd asked, *What if it doesn't save her?*

To this day, he remembered the stab of pain hitting him. She'd been teetering on the edge of falling apart. *Be strong. For your girl. For yourself,* he'd said while reaching for her hand to squeeze gently before handing her the water, all the time fighting the urge to haul her into his arms and promise everything would work out, but no one knew that for certain. When a nurse called him to say his patient was ready to see him, he'd left the woman before he made a mistake. He'd been there to donate bone marrow for a child with leukaemia as he'd been on the bone marrow donor registry since his brother was diagnosed and while waiting, he'd been checking on a patient.

'Likewise,' he now fibbed in answer to Caia. As he held open the door to the hall leading to the staff meeting room, a light citrus scent wafted his way, stirring him awake fast. Her wild, curly red hair held firmly in place with a wide black band made his fingers itch to set it free. For a moment, he thought if Caia Johnstone could get to him so easily, then perhaps it would be best if she didn't get the midwife position she was here to interview for. Of course, he was being irrational. Just because it had been a while since he'd last had a fling didn't mean his suddenly overactive hormones could get in the way of what the medical clinic required, which was a top-notch midwife. This woman came with excellent references. 'After you.'

'Thank you.' So polite and straight-backed, she stepped past him, making it clear she was here to get what she wanted. Like the midwife they'd interviewed yesterday. Only that one hadn't met expectations and would not be offered the job even if Caia also wasn't right for the position.

Except Lockie had a feeling she would turn out to be exactly who they needed, which would make things awkward if he didn't get this sudden yearning under control. Which he would. Just because Caia was beautiful didn't mean he should be lusting over someone who was here looking for a job. He really needed to step up his sex life—which was a bit of a desert these days. Then he wouldn't get all hot and bothered over a particularly attractive midwife.

He needed to focus on why Caia was here, because nothing else mattered. He'd thought about her often over the intervening year, wondering how things had turned out for her daughter. But it didn't feel right to ask now, especially as she didn't appear to recognise him. He hadn't removed his mask when he met her, so it was understandable that she wouldn't. 'Have you finished at Parnell Midwifery? Or are you still covering for someone?' From her application, he knew she had a temporary position there.

'I finish at the end of this week.'

'Have you enjoyed working there?'

One eyebrow rose elegantly. 'I thought I was to be interviewed by all of the partners.' Nothing sexy about that less than subtle poke.

'Just making conversation in case you're nervous before going in.' She looked anything but. Again, he was overreaching with Caia Johnstone with absolutely no reason to do so. She might be a stunning woman, but at the end of the day, he wasn't on the lookout for anything more than a casual fling, and that wasn't happening with a staff member. Even if they didn't take Caia on, he wouldn't follow up with how intense she made him feel, because something about her suggested he might not be able to let go easily, and he couldn't let that happen.

Marg had died by suicide three years ago. He was not prepared to love again. The loss of his wife had been beyond painful and loaded him with guilt. Deep down he knew it hadn't been his fault, but that didn't stop him thinking he should've known what Marg intended. Her parents had suffered the same guilt too, and that had made him feel even more responsible.

'I'm fine.' Caia's mouth tightened as though she was telling herself that as much as him.

Maybe not so fine after all? Did this position mean a lot to her? Her CV listed excellent references from previous employers, including from Parnell MC. But there was something going on behind her confident approach. Despite how she knocked his sanity beyond the park, he could sense it. He hoped everything had gone well at the children's hospital and her daughter had recovered well. 'Good. I don't like making people nervous. Through here.' He indicated the room they were going into, and held his breath so her perfume didn't taunt him again as she stepped past.

Caia strode further into the room, looking directly at Katie and Dave, the other partners, and nodded. 'Hello, I'm Caia Johnstone.'

Thank goodness that came out without a flicker of the worry twisting her stomach and tightening every muscle she had. If she didn't get this position, she was up the creek without any safe way back. She had to keep a roof over McKenzie's head and food in her little tummy. They hadn't been to hell and back for her to fail now.

'Pleased to meet you, Caia.' The woman stepped forward and shook her hand. 'I'm Katie Boys, and this is Dave Laurence.'

After shaking hands with both of them, she said, 'I'm looking forward to this.' Hopefully she didn't sound desperate in her attempt to be friendly. But neither did she want to appear aloof. That wouldn't win points, and she needed a lot of those on her side.

Lockie Roberts held out a chair. 'Take a seat.'

What was it about him that had her taking a second look? And a third. The moment he'd walked into the waiting room to collect her, she'd felt a sense of deja vu, which didn't add up as she didn't recognise him. Or did she? The rapid beating under her ribs seemed to say something different. She turned to study him. Then it came to her. Those intense eyes above a mask. He'd been at the water cooler when she'd gone to get a drink on the ward where McKenzie was waiting for her bone marrow transplant. She'd been a total mess, unable to stop shaking. When he'd asked if she was all right, she'd blurted out her fear without thought. Hell, she'd been beyond thinking anything except *what if McKenzie doesn't make it?* He'd told her to be strong, hadn't made inane comments, and almost seemed to understand what she was going through. Had he? She wasn't about to find out.

'Caia?' Lockie prompted her.

She shook her head fast. They'd cancel this interview if she didn't concentrate. 'Sorry.' Dropping onto the chair, she looked around at the people watching her, hoping no one thought she might be a bit loony. 'I— Sorry,' she repeated. What an idiot. If she blew her chance of getting this job because she'd been distracted, then she had no idea what she was going to do to keep life on track. There was little money in her bank account, and the mortgage payment was hanging over her head. Straightening her spine, she looked from Katie to Dave and finally at Lockie. 'I don't usually get sidetracked.' Now they'd want to know what caused her to lose focus, and she wasn't saying.

'Don't worry,' Lockie said as he took the remaining chair.

Did he remember her from that day and think she should acknowledge it when they had barely even spoken? She didn't intend discussing that time. It had been excruciating, and she wasn't going back there. She'd been fully focused on McKenzie while silently begging for the transplant to be a success. Nothing else had been important. Receiving a donor's bone marrow had been her girl's only chance for survival. The leukaemia had been getting out of control. The anaemia had worsened to the point McKenzie struggled to walk for more than a couple of minutes without becoming exhausted. Infections were standard as all natural immunity had disappeared when the white cells went crazy due to the lymphocytic leukaemia. 'Thanks,' she answered abruptly. Looking to the other partners, she asked, 'Where do you want to start?' *Let's get this over so I know where I stand.* Out on the street or about to be employed. The sooner she knew which one it was going to be, the sooner she could get on with whatever was required next.

As Lockie opened his mouth to answer, Katie took the lead, cutting him off. 'We've read your CV and the letters from previous employers, Caia. You come with a good reputation as a midwife. How about you tell us a bit about yourself. Things like why you chose to become a midwife, what you do when you're not working, and what your goals might be for the future.'

Caia felt her spine sinking, so she drew a breath and sat taller. It would be easier to answer direct questions, but if this was what it took to get what she required, then she'd do it. 'I like the positivity of midwifery. While there are occasions when a birth becomes difficult and a specialist is required, mostly it's a happy experience for everyone. Seeing a baby come into the world and mum's and dad's faces filled with awe takes my breath away every time. I like being a part of that.'

Katie nodded. 'Know what you mean.'

'I also enjoy working with women throughout their pregnancies, helping them overcome fears and making the most of the good moments.'

'What about when a birth goes wrong?'

The questions kept coming, and Caia relaxed further. This was how interviews went, and she had nothing to hide.

'I see you have a daughter,' Katie commented after a while.

'I do. McKenzie's five. She started school two months ago.' *And she's alive and well.* She glanced at Lockie and saw him smile. So he remembered.

'You're a solo mum,' he noted.

It said so in her CV. 'I am.' Had been from two months after McKenzie was conceived. 'Working and being a mother has its tricky moments, but I'm very lucky to have a friend who has two daughters of a similar age to McKenzie. She looks after my girl when I can't be there because of work.' *On rare occasions when there's no one to look after her and I get an overnight call out I have to take her with me and put her to bed in a spare bed at the clinic where I can keep an eye on her.* 'I'm not the only solo mum coping with work and family.'

'True.' Katie smiled. 'I'm raising two boys on my own, so know what you're up against.'

'That must be hard with the hours you put in here.' At least Katie would understand what she had to deal with and not hold it against her when it came to deciding if she got the position.

'I get round it.'

Glancing at Lockie, Caia thought from his relaxed manner that he knew she managed just fine.

Dragging up a smile, Caia said, 'I don't have much spare time, but when I do, I like reading crime novels.' She was usually too tired for anything else.

Dave laughed. 'Lucky you. I don't get to read a lot. It's the thing I miss most since becoming a parent of two kids—now teenagers.' His smile widened. 'Lockie's the odd one out. He gets to do whatever he likes in his time off.'

'Lucky blighter,' Lockie said.

So no kids? No partner? Caia wondered.

Lockie grinned, which further piqued her interest in him. 'I like getting together with Katie's and Dave's kids whenever I can, playing games and losing every time.'

Caia waited to see what these people wanted to know next. Volunteering info about herself willy-nilly was not something she did easily, and in this situation, it was even harder. She couldn't see past getting a permanent position and finally being able to relax a tad and put some money in the bank instead of having to count the dollars every day before she stopped at the supermarket for basics. She'd used up all her savings when McKenzie was ill and working hadn't always been viable.

Dave leaned back in his seat. 'So, Caia, what are you looking for if we take you on? What do you want going forward?'

'A settled life. A job that's not going to run out on me.'

'We're only looking for a permanent midwife. Part time isn't an option.' Dave told her.

She nodded. 'That's why I'm here. I'm not interested in anything but permanent.'

'Good to know.' As Lockie watched her, a smile crept across his mouth.

Kapow. Right to the stomach. How could he do that? She wasn't in the market for a man, and yet one small smile had her attention. Which was inappropriate of her at the moment. At any time, really, but she couldn't blame Lockie. She needed to focus on the interview. *You need this job more than anything.* Looking at the people sitting opposite her, she felt they'd be great to work with. None of them were pushing questions at her so fast she couldn't keep up. They seemed to want to let her be herself. Hopefully they didn't realise how desperate she was for this job. 'Is there anything else you'd like to know?' Might as well go for broke. She was walking out of here knowing she had given her all.

'How soon can you start?' Lockie asked.

Did he want her on board? 'Next week.'

He nodded and sat back.

She waited, because surely that wasn't the end of the interview? If it was, she was obviously out of the picture. She'd hardly warmed her seat in the time she'd been here.

'I'll fill you in a little about what we're doing. We've expanded our practise to include a birthing unit and midwife's office and are ready to take on new patients. We're also planning on adding a physio unit in the coming months,' Katie explained. 'There are other plans in the making, too, but they're not for discussion at the moment.'

'I understand.' They were obviously looking to go big. It would be good for patients to get follow-up treatment without having to go elsewhere. 'Sounds like an excellent plan, though I don't suppose the midwife's clinic will be busy at first.' That might mean fewer hours than she'd hoped for, though the ad read full-time, so she must have been wrong.

Lockie answered for the others. 'You'd be surprised. Between the three of us, we've currently got ten pregnant patients, and the general practise a couple of blocks away has more and is willing to refer their patients to our clinic, although it's entirely up to the women to choose where they go for midwifery care.'

'As long as they don't shift their files for all medical requirements over to your clinic, everyone's happy?' Caia found it easy to smile with these people, which said a lot. She was completely relaxed now. Which might not be wise. Too soon.

'You're on to it.' Lockie again. 'As it happens, our books are full. Other than maternity cases, we're not taking on any more patients so we can still give those we already have the attention required.'

His comment didn't surprise her. These three seemed grounded in their occupation and what was required to provide the best care possible. She had to get the job, and not just because she'd receive a steady pay packet. She wanted to work with them, to be a part of their team. 'I'm glad you said that. It's what our work is all about.'

Katie took over. 'We intend paying a salary to whoever we take on in the midwife's role. That way there're no weeks with little income if babies aren't arriving regularly, or not many women requiring a midwife, which happens at times.'

Being paid regularly would make for easier day-to-day expenses. 'Sounds perfect.' *Don't overdo it.* But she was being honest. It was ideal.

Lockie stood up. 'How about I show you around?' He seemed restless. Not good at sitting still for long? Or was he cutting this short, fidgeting about her wanting to work at this clinic? No. One short, intense time together over a year ago wouldn't cause that. Though her stomach was in a tangle whenever she looked at him, so she might be wrong.

'If there's nothing else any of you want to know about my application, then yes, I'd like that.' It would be less intense if Katie were to do the honours, but since she wasn't moving, Caia was stuck with Lockie.

'We've covered everything we wanted to find out. As you said, most information about your career's in your CV. This is more about meeting the woman behind the notes and seeing if she'll fit in with us.' Lockie held the door open for her.

She walked past him, holding her hands tight against her sides in an effort to ignore the heat emanating off him and causing unwanted tension to return to her stomach.

Before stepping out of the room, Lockie looked over his shoulder to Katie and Dave and saw them holding their thumbs up. So it was a yes from them. He raised his thumb just as enthusiastically behind Caia's back. She was exactly the type of person they needed as the clinic's midwife. Cool, calm and focused. She'd build up the midwifery clinic to a sustainable unit in no time at all. Women would flock to her for care during their pregnancies.

He was thinking about the practise, not how he was going to cope with Caia being in the same building day in, day out. The business came first, not his hormones. Anyway, he'd soon have them back under control along with an excellent midwife working for the practise. Still, he couldn't help wondering if she was going to be a problem. For some reason, in their two short meetings, she got to him too easily, and that didn't tie in with the fact he wasn't looking for a woman to share his life. He was too busy with the clinic and his role as head of the Auckland General

Practitioners' Association, not to mention being on the golf club committee, all of which filled many hours outside the practise. He'd been told more than once by the women he had his few-and-far-between flings with that he was selfish spending so much of his time working and not being there for any woman he was involved with. They didn't understand short-term when it came to a fling. There wasn't any other kind as far as he was concerned. He was not getting involved with another woman only to lose his head and heart again.

He led Caia along the hallway to the far end of the building. 'We started developing the building last year to include more facilities for the new clinics we mentioned opening over the coming year.'

'It's very modern,' Caia said as she entered the midwifery bay and looked around, her gaze landing on the new furniture. 'Nothing less than I expected, though. This is perfect. You all want to make the medical centre into something special.'

She'd nailed it. 'Yes, we do. We fully expect the people we employ to feel the same way.' He was querying how she felt about that. She'd come across focused and determined in her interview, but nothing like making certain.

Those fragile-looking shoulders tightened as she locked a firm gaze on him. 'Then look no further than me for your midwife.'

Nothing could stop the laugh that spilled out. 'You think?'

'I know.' No smile coming his way. But then, she had no idea what they all thought about her for the job. Katie and Dave appeared relaxed and pleased with Caia. And he felt that way when he wasn't overthinking how she made him tick on the inside. Time to get back on track before she disturbed him any further. 'Through here's the consult room with a bed and everything else required. This cupboard holds the Doppler, scales, fetal stethoscope and other essential equipment.'

Caia didn't even glance his way but instead looked around the room, giving the cupboards a thorough going-over. 'Looks like everything's been taken care of.' She wasn't one for idle chit-chat.

Not with him, anyway. 'I would certainly hope so.' What had she expected? That they wouldn't have the clinic organised and ready to go before employing a midwife? 'We're meticulous with the clinic's equipment, procedures and patients. And our staff,' he added pointedly.

'I can see that.' She stepped out of the room, but he didn't miss the heat flush through her cheeks. So she was embarrassed by her blunt comment.

Not as cool as she tried to appear, he mused. But then, being interviewed was hard work, especially if the job was very important to the interviewee. 'I assure you we are all focused on doing our best and more around here, and hope our midwife will be the same.'

Caia turned back, one eyebrow raised. 'If I get the position, then you can be assured I'll be the same as the rest of you.' This time there was a little rattle behind her words, as though she desperately needed the job and was afraid it wasn't going to happen.

'Let's go back to the others and talk some more.'

Without saying a word, she walked along the hall, her shoulders firmly back in place, and her spine once again straight as a ruler. But when they reached the waiting room where two patients were seated, she hesitated, looking directly at a young pregnant woman in the corner. 'Hello, I'm a midwife. Are you all right?'

'Yes. I'm waiting to see a nurse after these other people,' the young woman answered quietly. 'I don't have an appointment.'

Caia didn't look to him for approval but instead stepped across and hunched down in front of the woman. 'Are you sure you're all right? Why do you want to see a nurse?'

Tears leaked down the woman's face. 'Something feels wrong where my baby is, but I don't want to be a nuisance,' she insisted as her eyes widened in her pale face.

Caia took the woman's hand. 'You're not being

a bother. It's better we find out what's going on so we can help you and baby. What's your name?'

'Tami.'

'Okay, Tami, I'm Caia. How far along is your pregnancy?'

'Thirty-two weeks.'

Caia carried on calmly finding out what symptoms Tami was experiencing, not flapping over the potential problems behind whatever was causing the girl's discomfort. 'Tell me what feels wrong? Have you got a headache?'

'Yes. It was really bad all night and today. Sometimes my eyes are blurry.'

'Pain anywhere else?'

Tami rubbed her ribs. 'Here.'

Lockie wanted to step in and take over. He was the doctor on the scene, but he hesitated. Tami was trusting Caia with her problems, which said a lot for Caia. He stood aside, watching and listening, ready to do whatever was required should things turn bad in a hurry.

Caia looked up at him. 'Is there a room we can use? The midwifery room, perhaps?'

'Mine's closer.' A gut feeling told him to make the move as fast as possible. 'This way.' He took Tami's elbow to help her to her feet. 'I'm Lockie, one of the doctors. Let's go somewhere private and see what's going on, shall we?'

'It can't be anything terrible, can it?'

Caia had Tami's other arm in hand. 'We won't

know until we check you over, and it's best to do that as soon as possible for both of your sakes. Do you have a midwife?'

'No. I only arrived in Auckland from Western Australia two days ago, and haven't even finished unpacking, let alone sorting out things like finding a doctor and midwife.'

'Why not?'

'Too tired. The last few weeks were exhausting getting ready to move.'

'Have you got someone with you?'

'No. My boyfriend's working in the mines in outback Australia and won't be able to follow me back here for a month. I came home to be with my mum while I have my baby, but she's gone away for a week.' Tami didn't seem to understand Caia was distracting her so they could get her into his office and onto the bed quickly without any complications.

He had to hand it to her. She knew what she was doing. Hell, when she walked through the waiting room, she'd noticed something was wrong with Tami within seconds. He wasn't sure he'd have picked up on that. 'Shall I take the BP?' he asked her.

'Please.' She didn't stop to acknowledge he could rightfully take over as this was his practise and she didn't work here.

Yet. But she was going to. Despite his hesitancy about his earlier feelings, he knew this was one hell of a midwife. To let her go would be a travesty when they were trying to create a top-notch medical centre. 'I'll grab the Doppler while I'm at it.' Knowing the fetus's heart rate was imperative. Within moments, he was back.

Caia had Tami lying on the bed. 'Tami, I'm sure you know how this goes.' She placed a sheet over the woman's lower body. 'Can you raise your knees and spread them wide so I can examine you internally?'

Lockie handed her a pair of latex gloves from the box on the cabinet before pulling on a pair himself. 'Tami, I'm going to check your BP. Has it been normal throughout your pregnancy?'

'Yes.'

It wasn't now. 'One forty-seven over ninety-five,' he told Caia. Things were getting serious.

Her nod was abrupt as she continued with her examination of the vagina. 'All good here,' she said finally. Standing up, she removed the gloves. 'How's baby's heartbeat?'

'Slightly raised but nothing to worry about.' Yet.

'Tami, how painful is it under your ribs?'

'I broke two once, and this feels nearly as bad, but I haven't fallen or anything.'

Caia eyeballed him. 'Pre-eclampsia seems to be the problem.'

He nodded. 'I'll call an ambulance while you explain to Tami what's going on.' The young woman would no doubt prefer Caia stayed with her until the paramedics arrived than him. She'd barely taken her eyes off Caia the whole time.

Caia blinked. 'Thank you. Sorry, I do seem to have taken over, but it's natural for me when someone's having problems with their pregnancy.'

'I'd have been disappointed if you hadn't,' he told her with a wry smile. Both for him and for Tami.

CHAPTER TWO

DID THAT MEAN she had the job? Caia bit her bottom lip hard as she kept an eye on Tami. Were the partners interviewing anyone else? It would be hard if she had to wait days for others to go through the process and then finally learn the result. She'd be a zombie by then. There hadn't been a lot of sleep going on over the last couple of weeks anyway since Maryanne, the woman she'd been covering for, told her she was returning to work before the end of the month. The problem with agreeing to stand in for Maryanne until she came back had been not being able to procure another job until she knew exactly when the current one was going to finish.

In that respect, Maryanne let her down when she suddenly decided she was returning ASAP after taking more time than they originally agreed on. Not that Caia could blame her. She hadn't wanted to return to work when her maternity leave was up after McKenzie arrived in her life, but the day came when she had to. It had been the same when McKenzie's transplant worked and she could at last get out amongst people and go back to preschool. Then Caia had issues letting go of her fears of McKenzie catching a cold or some bug from her playmates. Fingers and toes crossed, Tami had been her good luck token, and she'd impressed Lockie enough to have a chance. Not that it was all in his hands. Surely Katie and Dave wouldn't leave it up to him alone.

'Hey, I hear we've got a mum and baby needing our attention.' A tall man dressed in the dark green-and-black ambulance service uniform strode into Lockie's room. 'I'm James, a paramedic.'

'Hi, James. I'm Caia, midwife, and this is Tami. She's thirty-two weeks pregnant and has pre-eclampsia. Suffering from severe headaches, high BP and pain under the ribs.' She handed over the notes she'd made covering the details.

'Thanks, Caia. Hello, Tami. Dr Roberts tells me we're taking you to hospital. Is that all right?'

'I suppose.'

'There's no one to go with her,' Caia told him. 'Her partner's working in Aussie, and her mother's away at the moment, though Tami's getting hold of her once she knows what's going to happen.'

'Then let's get you to hospital so you can find out the answer to that.'

The woman looked stunned. Everything was happening quickly. Caia made an instant decision. 'I'll call in and see you later, Tami.' It would be a fleeting visit as she had to collect McKenzie from her friend's house. As much as McKenzie liked staying with Izzy and the girls, Caia insisted on having McKenzie at home as much as possible so she understood where she belonged. When Caia was a child and her father disappeared out of her life, she'd spent a lot of time with neighbours or friends of her mother, feeling doubly deserted. She understood the need to feel centred, not adrift in her mother's comings and goings. *She* was McKenzie's rock and staying that way no matter what life threw at her. But it didn't mean she couldn't be there for others when they needed support if feasible.

'You don't have to do that,' Tami whispered, looking as if she'd like nothing more than having Caia visit her.

Lockie stepped in before Caia could utter a word. 'You're right—she doesn't have to, Tami—but seems Caia's got a big heart behind her midwife title. Make the most of it.'

That was going too far. He could have said she was following up to make sure Tami was going to be all right. Shooting him a tight look, she said, 'I know what it's like to be alone when something's out of whack with your pregnancy.' Now *she'd* gone and said too much. A look of surprise came her way, suggesting Lockie might think she'd do anything to get the job she was here for. 'I won't be able to stay long, though.'

James intervened. 'Think you can walk out to the ambulance, Tami? We'll take it slowly, but the sooner we get on the road, the sooner you'll have the attention you need.'

That was putting her in her place, Caia admitted. What she felt about Lockie had nothing to do with this scenario. Not now, anyway, and very likely never.

'I can walk,' Tami answered.

'I'll take an arm,' Lockie said in a *don't argue with me* tone directed at Caia rather than Tami as though he was reminding her that he was in charge here.

She wasn't about to argue with anyone. It wouldn't help get her the job she so desperately wanted, though hopefully she had scored some points with how she'd spotted Tami was in trouble, and how she'd dealt with it. Caia moved out of the way as Tami was helped to her feet. 'See you later.' She should have kept quiet, not opened her mouth and put her foot in it. Going to see how Tami was getting on meant time away from her girl, even if only a short while, and she loved nothing more at the end of the day than spending time with McKenzie. It was her dream time. Now she didn't even know how much longer she had to hang around here. Was her interview over, or did the partners have more questions?

'Would you want to come with Tami in the ambulance?' the paramedic asked Caia.

She winced. 'Sorry, Tami, but I'm in the middle of an interview, so I'll catch up with you later.'

Once again, Lockie took over. 'Technically your interview's over, Caia. If you want to go with Tami, that's fine.'

'My car's here. I'd have to follow.' Parking at the hospital wouldn't be easy.

'I can pick you up in half an hour and bring you back here for a final discussion about the position,' Lockie said. 'The practise will be closed by then.'

No pressure, Dr Roberts. There was no way she could get out of this without upsetting Tami, which was the last thing the woman needed right now. And it wouldn't help Caia's hopes of getting the midwife position if she baulked in front of Lockie now. 'Seems like we have a plan. You'll need my phone number to let me know when you get to the hospital,' she told him firmly. She wanted to add, *Don't be late*, but held back, not wanting to get out of favour. At least not until she knew where she stood with the partners and the job.

'Here.' He handed over his phone after tapping in her name.

After quickly adding her number, she passed him the phone and climbed into the ambulance.

'You'll want your handbag,' Lockie said from

behind her. 'I'll be right back. Don't leave yet, guys.' He loped off at pace.

Caia shook her head. She really was uptight about getting the job if she could forget her bag with her phone and bank cards in it. Taking a deep breath, she sat down out of the way of the paramedic and looked to Tami. 'How's it going? You feel a bit better now you've got help?'

'Sort of. I wish Mum was here. Or better still, Tobias.'

'Your partner?'

'Yes. He's going to be gutted he's so far away when things are going wrong.'

'Hey, hang in there.' She reached for Tami's hand. 'Let's get your mum back to Auckland so you've got family at your side. Can Tobias come home before his time's up?'

Tami grimaced. 'Yes, he can, but he doesn't finish his stint for another four weeks. *And* it takes forever to get to Perth from where he's working in the outback, followed by the long flight back to Auckland. I'll call him once I've seen a doctor and know what's happening. I'll call Mum then too.'

'Call her as soon as you get to hospital so she can make arrangements sooner rather than later.' It was odd that Tami's mother had gone away when her daughter had come home from Australia to be with her, but Caia wasn't asking why. All she hoped was the mother would turn up quickly.

She knew all too well it wasn't fun giving birth on your own, and having no one to share the special moment with when you held your baby for the very first time. McKenzie's father, Garth, had done a bunk the moment he learned he was going to become a dad. So much for loving her and wanting to get married. Apparently he never wanted to have children. They took too much attention. Something he'd forgotten to tell her in the beginning of their relationship. Her mother had been on a Caribbean cruise when she'd gone into labour. Not that her mother would've come home to be with her even if possible. Close didn't come near to what their relationship was. Distant was a better description. According to her grandmother it had been her mother's way of coping when her father up and left them when Caia was barely two. Her loving mother had become withdrawn and stayed that way ever since, allowing no one near. No wonder Caia had doubts about finding a genuinely loving man to share her life with.

'Caia, if I need a midwife after whatever happens, can I come to you?' Tami's voice was low and filled with tears.

'Of course.' Not sure where that would be, but she'd make certain Tami got everything she needed, including her attention. 'I was interviewing for the midwife's job at the GP's practise this afternoon and have to wait to learn if I got it. If not, we'll work something out, I promise.'

'Thank you so much. It's all a bit much dealing with everything when I only landed back home the day before yesterday.'

'I bet. But you're tough. You'll get through this.' She'd be there to make sure of it. It was the only way to go.

I'm outside the main entrance. Black sports car. Lockie pressed Send and pocketed his phone. He'd texted Caia when he left the practise to say he was on his way. She'd probably be waiting nearby. So much for keeping distant with her. He'd shown her around the new midwifery clinic without consulting the others. Then he'd put his hand up to come and collect her. All when she rattled him far too easily. Now it was going to get a whole lot harder to pretend she didn't exist. Not that he was about to give her the news they'd all agreed on back at the practise. He might be struggling to remain nonchalant with Caia, but he wasn't so far gone he'd spill the beans about that.

The passenger door opened, and Caia slid into the seat. 'Nice car.'

He hadn't seen her approaching. Maybe she wasn't getting to him as much as he thought. That had to be good. 'Hi. Yes, this is my one indulgence. I've always had a thing for sports cars. Once I qualified as a GP this car was my reward for all the hours I'd put in.' If that sounded selfish, so be it. He was entitled to have some enjoyment when time allowed.

'Lucky you.'

'What would your treat for yourself be?'

She tossed him a grin. 'A box of chocolates.'

He had a feeling that was quite likely. She didn't appear to be rolling in money. Her car was rundown, her clothes sensible and plain, and no signs of spending hours at a beauty parlour. But then, what did he know about women? His wife had turned out to be anything but what he'd believed. 'Everything all right with Tami?'

'Depends how you look at it. She's being admitted so they can monitor and decide whether to bring the birth forward or not. Her headache has lightened, but her blood pressure's still high. They're on to it, and Nick Graham's taken the case, so she couldn't be in better hands.'

'I agree.' Nick was a top-notch obstetrician he'd dealt with occasionally through work and knew well on the golf course. 'Thank you for all you've done. It's not as though Tami is your patient.' Yet.

'Wrong.'

Huh? Did Caia know she'd got the job?

'She asked me to be her midwife. I said yes, no matter what.'

'Of course you did.' Already he knew to expect no less of her. She had an air of decisiveness that suggested when she offered to help someone, it wasn't only for the next five minutes but for as long as needed.

'I'm not going out of my way to take a patient away from your clinic, but nor was I going to say no. The poor woman's feeling very lonely at the moment. That could change further down the track, but in the meantime, I'm there for her.' Caia made no apology. She was doing what she believed to be the right thing by Tami.

Which she was. So the sooner she found out what he, Dave and Katie had decided, the better. They could all relax—if she was happy with the outcome. He pressed the accelerator a little harder. Time to get back to the clinic and reveal their decision. And to get some fresh air that wasn't laden with her citrus scent.

'Thanks for the lift.'

'I'd hardly leave you stranded at the hospital after suggesting it was a good idea to go with Tami in the ambulance.'

'I hoped not, but I don't know you, do I?' She didn't mess around saying what was on her mind.

Nor did he. 'Rest assured I don't go back on my word.' Especially since Marg hadn't talked to him about what was going on in her head before taking her own life. He worked hard to be open and straightforward so people knew where they stood with him. One of the outcomes from those shocking years of trying to understand what Marg had done, and why.

Silence fell between them. Caia shoved a wayward strand of that fiery hair behind her ear as she stared out of the window.

'Have you applied for other positions besides ours?'

She drew a breath and turned to face him. 'No. I only learned my time was up at the other clinic ten days ago. There aren't a lot of midwife vacancies out there.' Her breasts rose on another intake of air. 'Plus I don't want to set up my own practise while McKenzie's so young.' There was a quiver in her voice as though she was trying to hide how important their job was to her.

He shouldn't have asked that particular question. Now he couldn't take away her worry until they returned to the practise where Dave and Katie were waiting for them. But he could apologise. 'I'm sorry. I shouldn't have asked what you might have in mind.' He was on the back foot and not happy with himself. He didn't like upsetting people.

'I suppose it's a natural question.'

One he suspected she had an answer for. 'Hang in there, Caia. When we get to the clinic, the others want a word with you. We all do.'

'Fine.' Her fingers plucked harder at her skirt. This position *was* important to her.

'Stop doing that or you'll pull a thread,' he said in an attempt to lighten the air between them.

'Not likely.' But she crossed her arms under her breasts and continued to stare out the window.

Thankfully they were almost there. He needed space to breathe. It was impossible to ignore Caia. Her eyes had that same suck-him-in thing going on he'd noticed at the children's hospital and were again putting him off balance. She created a deep need within him to let go and have some fun, to take a chance on finding a woman who wouldn't complain about the long hours he put in at work and other places. But that was crazy. She wasn't even looking at him, which kind of said she didn't feel the vibe between them he'd thought was there. Or she had the power to turn away because she wanted to. At the children's hospital, her focus had been internal, her daughter and what they were going through. Today she was all about getting the midwife's position. Nothing was distracting her. That had to be a good sign about how she approached her work.

Obviously the transplant had worked if the child was going to school. He'd sometimes wondered if the girl been the recipient of the bone marrow he'd donated, but she wasn't the only child waiting for a transplant that day, or that week, in fact. If she had been, did he want to know now that Caia was going to be working with him? It could be a complication to their workplace relationship. He wouldn't want her being overly grateful or asking him to meet her daughter because of what he'd done.

More likely he was completely wrong, and Caia and her daughter had nothing more to do with him than her position in the practise when she accepted the role. He knew she would. There'd been a moment of desperation in her voice when she said there weren't many positions available.

After pulling up in the clinic car park, he turned off the engine and opened his door.

Caia was out before him, heading for the front door, obviously in a hurry to know what was happening.

'Caia, wait up. Everything's going to be fine.' Yes, he was out of place saying that without the others around, but he couldn't stand seeing the worry in her tense shoulders.

She stopped, turned to look at him, worry clouding her eyes. 'I hope so.'

Her worry made him feel protective of her. But he couldn't put her out of her misery yet. It was a partners' decision, and therefore they all had to tell her the result. 'Just relax, will you?'

She blinked, slapped at her cheek as a lone tear snuck out of the corner of her eye. 'I'm trying to, but it's not one of my strong points.'

He could only smile and lead her inside, locking the door behind them as the practise was closed for the day.

'Come in, Caia,' Dave said as they approached

the room where they'd interviewed her. 'How did it go with the woman you went to hospital with?'

Caia quickly filled them in while looking uneasy, as if she desperate to know if they were going to employ her and not sure what he meant when he'd said everything would be fine.

'Thank you for doing that, Caia,' Katie said when she'd finished. 'You didn't have to, but I'm sure Tami was grateful to have someone go to the hospital with her.' She sat beside Caia.

The chairs had been moved to a more casual placement now that the interview was over. Lockie sat the furthest from Caia, needing the space and wanting to see her reaction to the news even though he'd already hinted at what it would be.

Katie took the lead. 'Caia, even before you noticed Tami had a problem and helped her and then went to hospital with her, we had already made up our minds about the midwife's position.'

Caia held her breath. Lockie had told her to relax, but she could've read him wrong. Until she heard she'd got the position for real and signed a contract, she wasn't going to feel relieved.

'It's yours. If you want it, that is.' Katie then told her what the salary would be.

She had a job. Not any old job but one at a clinic where what she'd seen here resonated with her need to be the absolute best at what she did.

'Hello, Caia? You still with us?' Lockie asked with a wide smile splitting his face.

She shook her head to clear her mind. She had the job she really wanted. Life was looking up. 'Thank you all so much. I am more than pleased to accept the position. As long as we agree on the details.'

Dave gave a serious nod. 'We did mention salary and holidays before, and after three months, when you'll have had the chance to get to know us and our patients, we'll have a brief discussion to assess an increase in salary.'

The day just got better. 'Thank you again.' She should've asked how much more, but that would sound greedy—or desperate. 'I can't wait to get started.' Everyone laughed like she'd made a joke, but she was serious. 'I mean it. I'm lost when I'm not working. Except when I'm with McKenzie. She keeps me on my toes.' Filled her with love.

'Motherhood does that,' Katie agreed. 'Once we've signed the contract, I'll open a bottle of bubbles to toast our success.' A frown appeared on her forehead. 'Would you like a drink?'

Absolutely. 'A small one would be lovely. I have to drive home afterwards.' She'd better call Izzy and explain why she was running late. Not that Izzy would mind, but she couldn't wait to share her news.

After she signed the employment contract, glasses of bubbles followed with everyone saying, 'Welcome aboard Caia.' She hadn't felt this good in a long time. Then she glanced at Lockie, and heat pinged in her stomach. How did he do that? She wasn't interested in him. Just because he could wind her tighter than a ball of string didn't mean she intended getting to know him on a personal level. He was now her boss, and she didn't need another man letting her down. Anyway, he'd said he led a very full life, so there'd be no spare time for a girlfriend by the sound of it. That was something else she didn't want—a man who didn't have time for her and McKenzie. McKenzie was not growing up learning what it was like to have her father figure walk away from her. Never. Caia would remain single until McKenzie was old enough to be setting up her own life as she chose.

'You're more relaxed than you've been so far.' Lockie stood beside her. 'You got what you wanted?'

'More than I expected, actually.' The increase in the salary was a huge bonus. So were the fixed hours in the clinic per week over and above the normal clinics and call-outs. More time away from McKenzie, but she was going to make that work by running clinics in school hours whenever possible.

'Good. Nothing like happy staff to make coming to work more enjoyable.'

For the first time since arriving for her interview, she laughed. 'I'm liking this more and more.'

Twenty minutes later, Lockie headed out to his car. The celebration had been short and sweet, and now he'd go home and relax some more.

Caia had the boot of her car open, and she was hauling out the spare wheel.

He veered in her direction. 'Problem?'

'Flat tyre.' She leaned the wheel against the side of the car and dug in the boot again for the jack tool.

'Let me take care of it.'

'I'm fine. Done it before.'

'I'm sure you have, but I'm not standing around watching you change the tyre on your own.' His parents had instilled manners in him and his brother from the get go, and he wasn't changing even if Caiasiad she didn't need his help.

A phone beeped. Caia delved into her bag.

'Saved by the bell,' he quipped, and got on with loosening wheel nuts before putting the jack in place to lift the car.

'Hey, Izzy. Sorry I'm running late. I meant to call you, but things got away from me. You won't believe it. I've got the job. Okay, so you thought I was in with a good chance, but you're my bestie. You have to think that.' Caia laughed, a deep laugh that made the skin on his forearms lift. 'I'll be there ASAP. Got a flat tyre to fix.'

'No, you don't, Caia,' Lockie retorted.

'That was one of my new bosses, Izzy. He's taken over with the tyre. Yeah, okay, for once I'll do as I'm told. Got to go. Tell McKenzie Mummy's on the way.' Her voice held soft notes whenever she mentioned her daughter. A true mum to the core. She rang off.

Lifting the flat tyre off the axle, he said, 'Do you remember that day we were at the water cooler?' He needed to get this topic out of the way or it was going to hang between them forever.

'Yes.'

'You said your daughter was loving school, so I presume she had a good outcome from her transplant?' Or she wouldn't be mixing with other children, surely?

'Yes, she did. I still pinch myself every day to make sure I believe it. It's the best possible outcome.'

That he could understand. 'What a relief that must've been. I've wondered how it all went for you both and am glad to hear your news.' Swapping the wheels over, he tightened the nuts back in place before lowering the car onto the tarmac.

'It was ALL.'

Acute lymphatic leukaemia. Same as Harry, his brother, had, and he'd never looked back after his transplant nearly thirty years ago. Of course, there were times when the family still worried, like when Harry got the flu or some other bug doing the rounds, but that probably would never change.

'You all right?' Caia asked. 'You've gone pale.'

He nodded. 'I'm fine.' Time to get away and calm down. He stood up. 'There you go. All fixed, but you need to get the tyre repaired ASAP in case you get another flat.'

Her eyes rolled in a derogatory way. 'Of course.'

'I guess you know that.' Idiot. Now she'd think he was acting superior.

'I do.'

'There's a shop two roads along from here. In case there isn't one close to where you live,' he added to show he wasn't trying to tell her what to do. If he wasn't too late.

She nodded. 'Thanks for doing this.'

'No problem.'

Finally she smiled sweetly—and sent his gut into spasms of need. 'I'll see you in a couple of weeks, then.' After getting into the car, she started the motor and drove away without looking back.

He stared after her even once the car disappeared around a corner. Why did she wind him up so fast? The first time he came in contact with her, she'd been vulnerable, and he'd wanted so badly to help her. Today she'd been strong and focused on why she was here, and he'd still wanted to be there for her, to support her in those moments when she was worried.

It really wasn't going to be easy to ignore Caia when he'd see her most days of the week.

CHAPTER THREE

CAIA WALKED THROUGH the main entrance of North Shore Medical Centre and headed down to the midwifery rooms, head high and back straight, grinning like a toddler with a yo-yo. Woo hoo. The beginning of her first permanent job in over two years, since McKenzie became ill, and she couldn't wait to get started. Day one working here and she couldn't have been happier. Bring on pregnant women and their excited families and friends. That's what midwifery was all about—except on the days when everything went to hell. Those days made her wish she'd become a bus driver, but they were few and far between the wonderful experiences she had with this work.

'Hi there, Caia.' The deep, gravelly voice that had haunted her sleep every night since her interview came from the main reception room. 'Welcome aboard.'

'Morning, Lockie. I've come in a little early to arrange my room as I'd like it.'

'Fair enough.'

'Later on, if there's time before my first patient, I'll pop along to the maternity hospital and introduce myself to whoever's around.' Doing that would help take away the feeling of being watched closely she felt in any new situation, something that went back to school and being called out by the headmistress for some misdemeanour or another while she was in the halls with her friends and peers. Getting into mischief had been her way of making sure she wasn't ignored, as her father had done to her. As she grew older, she realised it wasn't winning her any points in the friends circle, so she'd sharpened her wits to work at making genuine friends and keeping them after everyone left school. Then along came Garth and all his promises of love and forever, and everything changed. She was happy, believed she'd found the man of her dreams. She was so excited to tell him she was pregnant, only to have the mat pulled from under her when he said he never, ever, wanted children. He said unless she got rid of it, he was out of their relationship. But she wouldn't have an abortion. That was the same as leaving her child, like her father had done. Garth was gone that night, never to contact her again, increasing her belief that no man would want her forever, would love her for who she was. Nor did she want McKenzie to ever confront the same lesson, seeing her mother being left time and again by men she brought into their lives and feeling that she'd been abandoned too. Hence the walls around Caia's heart.

Lockie interrupted her train of thought, bringing her back to here and now with, 'You need to meet the rest of the crew here first.'

'I'd love to meet the crew. Everyone I met when I was here for my interview was so friendly, though I know full well that when I get down to business, those same people will be keeping an eye on how I go about my work.' She grinned slowly. 'Can't say I blame them. We all like to know our colleagues are up to scratch.'

'After the way you stepped up for Tami, I doubt anyone has doubts there. Word got around fast.'

'You didn't have anything to do with that, did you?'

'It wasn't exactly a secret.'

She didn't know what to say, so kept quiet as per normal when not surrounded with her closest friends. She also needed to be careful around this man. No way did she want him thinking he'd raised her interest. That wouldn't be wise. He was one of her bosses. Anyway, these days she wasn't into having flings no matter how short or fun they were.

'Come through to the smoko room, where everyone who's on duty this morning will be grabbing coffee like there's about to be a shortage.' He headed down the hall, not waiting to see if she followed.

Obviously she was meant to, so she obliged. Anyway, coffee sounded good. She'd been a caffeine addict since she started studying for her midwifery degree while working five hours a night packing shelves in a warehouse. Some days the only thing to keep her awake through lectures had been coffee. It couldn't have been too bad, though, as she aced the exams, coming top of her final year. It was her biggest moment ever, and she'd been so proud. Even her mother had showed up for the awards ceremony *and* given her a hug and a return ticket to Brisbane, where Izzy was working at the time.

Lockie waved her into the staffroom with a light smile. 'Hey, everyone. This is Caia Johnstone, our new midwife. Not all of you have met her yet.'

Caia felt good when everyone smiled and welcomed her aboard.

'How do you take your coffee?' Lockie asked.

'White with one.'

'Make the most of it.' A nurse sitting at the table grinned. 'Lockie's not known for running around after the hardworking crew. I'm Val, by the way. Grab a seat.'

Plonking her butt down, Caia looked around at everyone, recalling the few names she'd learned the day of her interview. 'Glad to be here. I need to get up to scratch on where everything's kept and that sort of thing.'

'Shouldn't be too hard. We keep everything fairly straightforward,' Val told her. 'But after coffee, I'll come with you in case you have any questions. I know you were shown around when you had your interview, but that's never enough, is it?'

'Definitely not.' A mug of coffee appeared on the table in front of her.

'Here you go.' Lockie stepped back quickly. 'I'll catch up later to see how you're doing.'

'Sure.' Thought he had plenty of time before his first patient. Didn't he like sitting around yabbering with the crew? Disappointment rose when she had no right to feel that way. She was a staff member, not his number one midwife. Or anything more important. But despite sitting at the table with the two nurses and two reception staff the room felt empty the moment he left. Nothing was adding up. Lockie meant nothing to her, other than a colleague. A man with eyes that drew her in whenever they sought her out, eyes that set rays of heat churning her inside out. She'd been in the building barely ten minutes and already he had her in a pickle. Maybe it was time to get out and have some fun. Having sex might do the trick and settle her hormones down for a while, but they were so out of practise she'd probably make a fool of herself.

Or could she put them to use with Lockie? That was a definite no-no. She didn't believe in getting too close to anyone she had to work with. It could only end badly, and she needed this job more than she needed sex. Sex didn't fill the pantry, buy McKenzie's school uniform, pay school fees or buy a new dress for her doll. *Stop being so melodramatic.* First day on a new job was always unsettling until she began to fit in with the systems and staff, but she was being a bit OTT at the moment. Raising her mug, she said, 'I'm happy to be here and hope to get along with you all.'

'Of course you will. We're a great lot.'

'We're glad you're here to carry some of the load, if only with the pregnant patients. I reckon you'll be busy before you know it,' Joanne, the other nurse, said.

Busy was part of the deal and the downside to any job when it came to being there for McKenzie, but she'd cope. 'Nothing I haven't done before.' The coffee was more than good. Taking another mouthful, she said, 'As for the coffee maker, he knows what he's doing.'

Everyone laughed. 'Good luck with getting Lockie to make you a brew often. He usually comes in and downs ours if we're called away.'

'I'll make sure to finish mine before leaving the room.' Caia relaxed further. Everyone seemed easy to get along with, which was all she wanted.

'I understand you've got a daughter,' Val said. 'Is she at school?'

'Yes, year one, and absolutely loving it. After

school, she goes home with my friend who's a teacher there and her two girls, so I don't have to worry if I get caught up with a birth.' She'd be lost without Izzy and her husband, Brett.

'Good to have everything sorted, isn't it?' Val drained her mug. 'My husband works from home, which makes life easier for me when I'm caught up here. Right, I'll go get on with my list of chores. When you're done with your coffee, come and find me so we can go through everything more thoroughly.'

'Thanks.' She hadn't covered everything with Lockie the other week, and she did need to follow up on making sure she knew exactly where all the equipment was kept and arrange it how she preferred. Better than being found wanting when a problem occurred too fast.

Thirty minutes later, after going through things with Val, she went to tell Lockie she was going to the maternity hospital. He was in his office looking through patient records for the previous months. His smile was tight, nothing like his other warm, sexy smile that drifted through her dreams most nights. 'Problem?' she asked.

'Over the past months, we haven't had a lot of new pregnancies,' he said.

'Why's that? We're in a suburban region with many young couples. I'd have thought it was the ideal location for maternity facilities.'

'You're right, but there's been a shortage of

midwives lately, two of whom are having babies. Ironic, I know. But that's life. I'm guessing pregnant patients have gone further afield for a midwife. Our aim is to bring them back in.'

'Hopefully things turn around once people hear about the new clinic.' The idea of not being busy was a worry.

Lockie nodded. 'I'm sure they will. The patient numbers do go up and down on a regular basis, but not so much up at the moment. You scored Tami for our practise. Seems you're already growing the practise. Not that we're here to steal patients off other midwives,' he added hastily.

'I wouldn't do that. I don't abide by it. It's unprofessional.'

'Relax, Caia. I wouldn't be pleased if that's what you did. I saw how you were with Tami. It's no surprise she wanted you as her midwife. She's now registered as a patient with our general practice as well as with the midwifery department.'

'Thought the general register was closed.'

'Her mother's a patient of Katie's, so we made an exception.'

'I'm glad. Tami's lovely.'

Lockie's eyebrow rose. 'And that has what to do with being our patient?' He grinned.

'Always good to have decent people to treat.' Damn, he was easy to talk with. Too comfortable. So much for holding back and not reacting to his smiles and husky voice and that fit body, which had her fingers itching to touch him everywhere. Yes, everywhere, up, down and all around. 'I'd better get moving.' Get the hell out of here before Lockie clicked onto the fact he was turning her on.

'Have you finished looking around to see where everything's kept?'

'Yes. Val gave me a tour.' It wasn't exactly a large building with lots of rooms and cupboards to go through. 'I feel comfortable with everything.'

'Okay.' Was that disappointment clouding his face?

Couldn't be. It wasn't his job to show her around. He had more important things to do, and right now she didn't need to follow him around like a puppy waiting for a bowl of food. Except it wasn't food she wanted from Lockie. It was that body devouring her mind and winding her tight. Could Lockie be feeling the same intense sensations about her, and that's why she felt so pulled to him? No. She was daydreaming. But what if he was? He was a man. She was a woman. It was natural. Throw in that it'd been two years since her last fling. Before McKenzie became ill, in fact. No wonder she felt this way about a sexy man. It was time to let loose, if her body remembered what to do. Judging by the sensations filling her now, it mightn't have forgotten much after all. 'I'm going to take a look around the maternity hospital now.'

'I'll come with you and introduce you to the head nurse.' Lockie took her elbow, then hurriedly dropped it.

What could she say? He was the boss. 'Sure.' Trying hard not to rub her elbow where he'd briefly touched it, she followed him out of the room. Eyes forward, no ogling the man rearranging her thoughts on not getting involved with any male for a while to come.

'Caia, who looks after McKenzie when you are at a birth overnight?' Lockie asked once they were in the car.

She'd told them at the interview she had everything under control. But this was a man who cared about other people. She'd seen it with Tami that day. And again when he'd taken over changing her tyre. 'She stays with the friend I mentioned during my interview. They're McKenzie's second family. Everyone's close, and it's so special. I'm very lucky.'

'Sounds like McKenzie is too. What about your family? Don't they live nearby?'

Change of subject required. Except she couldn't find it in her to avoid answering Lockie's question. For the first time since Garth hightailed it out of her life, she wanted to be up-front about her family. Which showed how much Lockie got to her. 'My mother lives in Christchurch. I have no siblings. Nor a father.' Nothing more to say. As it was, that was too much info to give out when she didn't really know Lockie, but she hadn't been able to hold back. Which was odd in itself. Because he was good-looking didn't mean she had to share her heartache with him.

Lockie glanced at her. 'What about McKenzie's father? Is he on the scene?'

'You don't hold back, do you?'

'Not when I'm getting to know someone I'll be rubbing shoulders with daily.'

'What?' This was interesting. Maybe he was getting the same vibes off her as she was him. Was that why he'd asked about McKenzie's father? No. She had to be wrong. He was merely showing interest in the newest staff member, so she'd better open up a little rather than risk appearing reluctant to talk about herself. It didn't do to feel awkward around the bosses. 'He did a bunk the moment I told him I was pregnant. Said he was going home to Wales. For all I know, he could still be living in Auckland, but neither do I care. He's a waste of air.'

After pulling into the facility car park, he stopped the car and turned to her. 'You deserve to be treated better than that.'

'I agree.' Time to bury this conversation. She'd shared more than enough. Glancing at her watch, an heirloom from her grandmother that she treasured even if it was outdated, she said, 'I need to get a wiggle on or I'll be late getting back for my patient.'

Inside the updated building, Lockie headed down the corridor. 'Janice won't waste your time. She likes to get on with things and not mess around.'

Then they should get along fine.

'Morning, Janice,' Lockie called to a middle-aged woman walking towards them. 'Thought I'd formally introduce Caia to you before she gets started.'

'Hello, Caia. I'm glad you're working along the road. We need you plenty.' She held out her hand.

'So I heard.'

'In case you're wondering, that's not why you got the position,' Lockie interrupted. 'A shortage of midwifes or not, we wouldn't take on just anybody.'

She could handle an ego boost any day. 'That's what I want to hear.'

'Thought it might be.'

Would he please stop delivering those sensual smiles? They moved the floor beneath her feet, making her unstable. 'Thanks for the ride, Lockie.'

Janice said, 'I'll give you the tour. Catch up later, Lockie.'

'Oh, all right.' He looked taken aback. Not used to being pushed aside? 'Hang on, I have to wait for Caia since I drove her here.'

'It's barely half a kilometre, and I've got two perfectly good feet. I'll see you back at the practise.' She didn't want Lockie hanging around any longer. He took up all the spare air and left her light-headed.

'Fine.' With that, he left.

Caia sighed. Would she see so much of him in the general practise that she'd never get her head straight about the way he turned her on so fast?

'This is where you'll see the patients who come in for check-ups.' Janice pushed open a door and led the way into the small room. 'You'll find everything you need in those cupboards. The linen basket's behind the bed.' She filled in all the details Caia might need before taking her to the birthing units and the rooms where mothers stayed for one or two nights after their baby was born, depending on how they were managing. 'And that's it. I'm sure there's nothing you haven't worked with before, but if you have any questions, come straight to me. I'm always available.'

Caia said, 'Good to know. Thanks for showing me around. I like to get a good look at where I'm going to work before I start.'

'Totally understandable. And professional.'

That might a bit over the top, but she'd take the compliment. No such thing as too many of those.

On Friday morning, Caia headed straight to her rooms at the practise. She'd picked up coffee to go at the cafe over the road so she didn't have to waste time in the break room. Her first patient was coming on her way to work.

'Matilda, how are you?' She'd seen Matilda while covering for the midwife at her previous job and wondered why she was here when her previous midwife had returned to work. 'I wasn't expecting to see you.'

'I hope you don't mind, but I want to swap to you. You make me feel so comfortable when you're checking me over, and I want to have you for the rest of my pregnancy.'

Ouch. Tricky. But it came with the territory. Some patients didn't gel with their midwife, usually first pregnancy cases who were uncomfortable about not knowing what lay ahead and asked endless questions or moved on to another midwife. Nevertheless, she didn't like taking on a colleague's patient without consulting her first. 'Have you talked about this with the other midwife?'

Matilda looked slightly embarrassed. 'I told her last week. She was okay about it. She said you were a great midwife, and if you made me feel better about what was ahead, then I should do what I felt was right. Is that okay? I don't want to upset anyone, but I am so much more relaxed with you.'

Relieved, Caia said, 'It's fine. It happens sometimes, and a patient's well-being comes first. I'm happy to still get to work with you.'

'I was worried I'd cause trouble. It's hard enough waiting for my baby to arrive without feeling awkward about my midwife as well.'

'It's all good. Take a seat, and I'll check your blood pressure before examining you internally.' The baby was due in eight weeks. Matilda getting impatient for it to be over so she could hold her infant in her arms wasn't unusual. First babies did that to their parents. And that was only the beginning. There were the busy two-year-olds, the action-packed threes, the know-it-all fours. McKenzie had missed out on the know-it-all stage since she'd been so ill. Making up for it now, though, Caia thought. School was her favourite place to be. She soaked up learning faster than she'd learned to drink out of a bottle as a toddler, and that had been quick enough. 'Did you have a scan last week?'

Matilda beamed at her. 'Yes, and we're having a boy. Jacob Thomas Grenville.' Her elbows dug into her sides as she talked, excitement spilling out of her eyes. 'Bring him on. Or should I say out?'

'Not too soon,' Caia warned with a smile. 'Stick to nature's plan of forty weeks to give him the best start in life.'

'I know, but we can't wait to meet him.'

'I'm a wet blanket.' Caia grinned. 'Goes with being a midwife.'

'What made you decide to be one?'

'Because I love babies and doing all I can for women to have a great experience throughout their pregnancy and birthing.' *Because I want to be there for people when I couldn't always rely on others to be there for me, Izzy and Brett being the exceptions.*

'You're really good at what you do.'

'That's enough from you,' she said with a false growl. 'I don't want to get big-headed.' It was nice to get a compliment, though. 'Right, BP's good. Get up on the bed and I'll check you over.'

Minutes later, Caia tossed her gloves in the bin. 'Jacob appears to be quite happy in there. No problems with anything.'

Matilda sat up and pulled her knickers up, followed by baggy track pants. 'That's great news. I know I shouldn't worry, but I always do before an appointment with you.'

'You're normal. You might be used to it by the time you have your sixth baby.'

Matilda's eyes widened. Then she grinned. 'I don't think so. Imagine having six kids running around driving me crazy all the time.'

'I can't begin to think what that'd be like,' Caia admitted. 'One's enough to keep me on my toes.'

'You've got a child?' Surprise blinked out at her.

Why wouldn't I? 'Yes, I have a daughter. Best

thing to ever happen to me.' Which was completely true.

'That's lovely. I guess you know what you're talking about when explaining things to your patients, then.'

'On a practical level, yes, I do, but trust me, all midwives have a very good idea about what's going on, regardless of whether they've had a baby themselves or not.'

'Sorry, I wasn't thinking when I said that. I didn't mean to sound scathing of midwives who haven't been through pregnancy.'

'I'm sure you didn't, Matilda.' She hoped not. 'I'll book in your next appointment. Then you're set to go.'

'I'll see you more frequently now that there's only eight weeks before show day, won't I?'

'Every two weeks until the thirty-sixth week, then weekly. I'll need to keep an eye on baby's growth and your health. Monday fortnight for your next visit work for you?'

'Perfect.'

'Are you happy to come to the maternity facility around the corner to have your baby?'

Matilda nodded. 'Yes. My husband will be with me.'

'Of course. You can bring your parents or a friend too.' If it hadn't been for Izzy, she'd have been alone when McKenzie was born, something else she'd be forever grateful to Izzy for. The list kept getting longer, not shorter, because there wasn't much she could do for her well-organised friend except babysit when she and Brett went on their date nights.

'See you in two weeks.' Caia sat at her desk to update Matilda's notes.

Knock, knock. Lockie stood in the doorway. 'You got a moment?'

'Sure.' She couldn't think of anything she'd done wrong, but since she'd started, it was Lockie who always seemed to be keeping an eye on her. It was nearly impossible not to stare when he leaned his butt against the unit of drawers, his legs looking longer than ever.

He looked serious, making her worried. 'Tell me to back off if you want, but I was wondering if you'd have dinner with me tonight. It won't be a late night as you've got a wee one to get home to. Think of it more as a catch-up on how your first week's panning out.'

'Why not do that here?' She hadn't done something wrong. Her shoulders dipped. Phew.

'We could, but we've both got to eat, so I figured a decent meal at the same time wouldn't go amiss.'

Then it dawned on her what he'd asked. 'Really?' She was struggling to get her head around his invitation. Lockie might—did—get her in knots all too easily, but going out together seemed a bit much. Although she'd like to go out for a meal with him, it might end up being uncomfortable. Face it, it wasn't a real date if they were going to talk work. She didn't do rushing into any sort of relationship. Not even one that involved dining out and nothing else. Certainly not when every cell in her body was screaming for some fun. That was plain scary and intriguing all in one. 'Do you think it wise to go out together when you're my boss?'

'Wouldn't have asked if I thought there'd be a problem. For clarity, I have mentioned this to Dave and Katie. They have no problems with it.'

'Do you invite other staff members out on a date often?' The moment the question was out, she wanted to take it back. It was rude, but then, she was used to protecting herself no matter what. Except today, it didn't feel as though that's what she was doing. The truth was, she had no idea what she was feeling except maybe anticipation for some fun being out with a man and having a meal. But what if Lockie found her boring once he truly got to know her? What then? Things could get really uncomfortable.

He was watching her closely. 'Caia, if I've upset you, then I apologise. But I like that we've clicked, and spending time getting to know you better would be great. If that's not an option, then say so and I'll move on.'

To what? To whom? Damn, she was getting antsy. Lockie was right. They had clicked from the moment they met. Something in his eyes had snagged her and not let go since. As had his honesty. Also his sexiness. 'Okay, then, yes, I'd love to have dinner with you as long as Izzy's okay looking after McKenzie. I'll give her a call when I'm free. And you're right, I won't want to be late to pick her up afterwards.' Which meant no to spending time between the sheets somewhere. If it came to that, and really she knew it wouldn't. She was daydreaming. Sex was out of the picture with any man until she knew him better. That was assuming he'd still wanted to spend time with her afterwards.

'I'll pick you up at six thirty unless I hear that your friend can't have McKenzie.'

'You don't have my address.'

'Unless your CV was a forgery, I can find it.' He grinned. 'But you're right, it'd be better to ask you.'

Her knees were knocking. She needed to pull her head in and find the courage to tell him she'd changed her mind. Except she hadn't. Going out to dinner with Lockie might help get her new life underway. That meant stopping being reclusive, something that began when Garth left her and had grown deeper ever since, especially when McKenzie got sick and she worried about passing anything along. Now she had a permanent job. She was getting into a routine she hadn't known since McKenzie's illness and all the days and nights at her daughter's bedside waiting for her to recover. Going out for dinner to discuss work was a small step towards a settled life. Small? Not true. It was huge. The way Lockie fired up her body had nothing to do with small either. She'd have to focus hard on controlling her reactions when sitting at a table with him. Hopefully it would be worth it.

As Lockie walked away, another thought struck Caia. What the heck was she going to wear? Her wardrobe wasn't bursting with dresses or going-out outfits. Something else to ask of Izzy. *Her* wardrobe was like an upmarket clothing shop, and most dresses didn't get worn more than once or twice.

When her last patient for the morning left, she checked the time. Izzy would be on lunch break. Holding the phone tight, she wondered if her brain had made up the invitation. It seemed too good to be true.

'Hey, Caia, what's up?' Izzy asked.

'How's your day going?' A stalling tactic. She shouldn't have called her friend when she was uncertain of what she was doing.

'If you think running a classroom of five-year-olds is fun, then I'm having a ball.'

'That good, eh? You'll survive.' Izzy loved teaching the youngsters.

'I will. Now, what can I do you for? You don't usually call to check up on McKenzie but she's fine anyway, and so are my two. I'm guessing you're after something else.'

'Can't surprise you at all, can I? Can you have McKenzie for an extra couple of hours tonight?'

She was answered with a laugh. 'Not until you tell me what you're up to.'

Here we go. I'm about to get a grilling, but that's what best friends do. Especially Izzy. 'I'm going out to dinner.'

'A date,' Izzy hooted. 'A hot one, I hope.'

'Might be.'

'Don't tell me Dr Lockie's asked you out.' Silence fell. Izzy said, 'Okay, you can tell me.'

'Dr Lockie's asked me out to dinner. To discuss how my week's going,' she added hurriedly.

'Yay.' She could see Izzy fist-pumping the air. 'Awesome. I knew something was up. You looked so off-centre whenever his name came up. Is he hot?'

'It's late winter and cold outside.'

'In other words, yes, he's hot. Go girl. I'm excited for you. It's about time you got out and had fun.'

'As long as that's all I have.'

'You're on the pill. What can go wrong?'

He could break her heart or treat her as though she wasn't very lovable. 'I've told him I can't be late picking McKenzie up.'

'She can stay the night with us.' Izzy sounded excited, as though it was her going on a date.

'That's not happening. She comes first. Anyway, we might run out of things to talk about before the food comes out, and then Lockie will want to be on his way faster than I can imagine.' She should've turned him down, talked with him here over coffee. If things went wrong, then working here would not be easy.

'Caia, I'll say it again. Go and enjoy yourself. Who knows what might come of it? Lockie must be keen if he's asked you out during your first week on the job. Make the most of this. You deserve some fun, girlfriend.'

It was supposed to be about work, she reiterated to herself as moisture filled her eyes. 'Damn you, Izzy.' Her friend was right. She did deserve to let loose and have fun. If only she didn't get nervous and start looking for what could go wrong instead of sitting back and soaking up all the fun aspects of being with a hot man. With Lockie. He was more than hot. He was also decent. But did that mean he wouldn't up and walk away without a backward glance the second he chose? Going on past experience, she didn't have an answer to that.

'What colour outfit do you want to wear?'

Caia blinked. It wasn't too late to cancel with Lockie. 'I don't know about this.'

'Stop overthinking everything that could go wrong.'

Sudden laughter rolled up Caia's throat, the

tears gone in a flash. 'Damn you again. Am I that obvious?'

'I've got to go. The head wants a yarn. See you at my place when you knock off. We'll find the perfect outfit.' The line went quiet.

Damn you, Izzy. Where would I be without you?

Most likely going on a date in overworn jeans.

CHAPTER FOUR

'WHO ARE YOU?' one of the three young girls standing in the doorway demanded.

'I'm Lockie. Who are you?' Caia had texted asking him to pick her up at her friend's house.

'McKenzie Johnstone. Are you taking my mum out for dinner?'

So this was the little girl tearing Caia's heart into pieces that day at the hospital. To think he might've given her a second chance at life. Of course he was getting ahead of himself and more than likely wrong, but it would feel good if he had.

'I asked you a question.' The little girl had her mother's demanding way about her.

Swallowing a smile, he answered solemnly, 'Yes, that's me. I'm Lockie. Is your mum ready?'

'I think so.'

'You can do better than that, McKenzie. You know she is,' said a woman heading along the hall. 'Hi, Lockie. I'm Izzy, Caia's friend. She'll be right with you. Just dealing with a call from the maternity hospital.'

Hopefully not a call about a baby deciding to arrive early. It went with the territory for midwives—with many medical fields, including GPs—but he hoped tonight would be one time neither he nor Caia was interrupted. It was her first week on the job, and as far as he knew, none of her patients were due to deliver, but pregnancies had their own timelines.

'Relax. It isn't anything urgent.' Izzy wore a wide smile, belying what lay behind questioning eyes. 'Come on in.'

He suspected he was about to get a grilling. If this was Caia's best friend, she'd be wanting to know things about him he had no intention sharing. Not with her, anyway. But rather than appear offhand, he stepped inside as the girls moved back in a huddle, grinning at each other as though he'd given them a bag of lollies. 'Thanks for babysitting so we can go out, Izzy.'

'Not a problem. Just give her a good time. She deserves some fun in her life.'

Sounded like a warning to him. 'I'll do my best.'

Izzy locked a steady look on him. 'You'd better.'

Yes, ma'am. 'I don't intend on being a boring oaf,' he retorted, unused to being told how to date a woman.

'Hey, Lockie, sorry to keep you waiting.' Caia strolled along the hall as though she hadn't a worry in the world. Until he noticed how tight her shoulders were, and he knew it was all for show.

Out of practise in the dating scene? He couldn't imagine so. She was beautiful. As well as interesting. Any man in his right mind would want to spend time with Caia Johnstone. 'I only got here a couple of minutes ago.' In that time, McKenzie had quizzed him, and Izzy had laid down a line that he was meant to cross. Only she hadn't said by how far, so that one at least could be his and Caia's decision.

'Then let's go. But first…' Caia spun around. 'McKenzie, come here, sweetheart. This is Lockie, the man who's taking me out to dinner. Say hello.'

'I know who he is, Mum. I asked him.'

Caia chuckled. 'Why am I not surprised?' She looked to Lockie. 'Did you get a grilling about tonight?'

'You bet. I have to have you back in an hour or she'll report you missing.'

'No, I won't,' McKenzie yelled. 'I didn't say that.'

Lockie grinned. 'I'm teasing, McKenzie. I promise to look after your mum.'

McKenzie tapped his hand. 'You're naughty. But you can take Mummy out for dinner.'

There's a relief. 'Thank you.' He could get to like this little monkey with her frank stare.

Caia brushed a kiss on her daughter's cheek. 'Be good. I'll take you home later when Lockie drops me off, sweetheart.'

'I'm always good.'

Izzy opened the front door. 'Out of here, you two. Go enjoy yourselves.' She gave Caia a brazen wink.

Might've been wise to have stayed in the car and tooted to let Caia know he was here. That way her friend wouldn't have had a chance to crank up the tension already making itself felt within him. This was a dinner date, no more, no less. Or so he'd been telling himself from the moment Caia had accepted his invitation. There was nothing new about taking women to dinner, yet he'd never felt quite as tense. Caia was very attractive, but that had nothing to do with his current feelings. She was an enigma. Kind and gentle with her patients—and her daughter. She listened to people, not a common trait and one he appreciated. She must be tough, too, because dealing with McKenzie's illness with no family there to support her would've been beyond intense. She wasn't overly forthcoming about herself. When her ex walked away because she was pregnant, had she become cautious about letting anyone in? There was so much he wanted to find out, but he had to be patient or she'd turn her back on him permanently.

Finding out how well they could get along was

important. They needed to get along as colleagues and friends. Sitting down over a meal and chatting about this and that, they could let go the tension that arose between them at times, as long as Caia hadn't read more into it and didn't see the night out as a serious date.

Because for him, it wasn't a serious evening, more about relaxing and enjoying themselves. He *was* intrigued by Caia, but she mightn't care less about him other than as one of her bosses, which was really how it should be. He wasn't admitting she might tighten the need he already felt whenever around her and that he'd like to follow up with more dates. Problem there was that another person had to be considered in this—McKenzie. He would not be responsible for hurting her.

He'd always be grateful for his family. They were all there for each other no matter what life threw at them, the worst being when Harry had been diagnosed. It'd been a devastating time waiting for a bone marrow donor to be found and watching Harry's health decline daily. And still, while his parents were focused on Harry, Lockie wasn't ignored or forgotten. When they couldn't be there for him, his uncles and aunts or grandparents stepped in to look out for him. Because the family came from a long line of doctors, his grandfather and two uncles were medical specialists along with a cousin, Harry's illness had seemed particularly hard to cope with. All of them felt guilt for not being able to do anything to save Harry other than wait for the oncologists and pathologists to do their jobs. Everything turned out well. Harry was now a pathologist, and Lockie had donated his bone marrow twice to help others get the same wonderful outcome as Harry.

Caia tapped his arm. 'Are you going to be this conversational all evening?'

Shaking away the thoughts that had overtaken him, he led her to his car. 'I'll crank it up a bit if you like.'

'Absolutely. I've spent the last hour listening to McKenzie rabbiting on like there's no tomorrow and could do with some adult conversation.'

Opening the door, Lockie said, 'Nothing too serious, I hope.'

'You don't do serious?'

'Not after a long day dealing with any number of illnesses and injuries.' The last thing he needed was deep and too meaningful, though he did want to delve into what made Caia tick. Right now he decided that could wait until another time. Tonight was about relaxing and making the most of her company. He'd also cover the subject of work since that was the reason he'd given for asking her out. It hadn't been a lie, but he hadn't been entirely truthful. He'd also wanted to spend time with Caia. That was rare, considering how many hours he put into the practise and the GP association's board. Then there were the golf club committee he was on and the games he played with his mates. Any spare moment was usually taken up with mundane chores around his home. So time with Caia was important even if he had no idea where it might lead, if anywhere at all. It wasn't as though he'd forgotten the women he'd got close to who'd complained he never had enough time for them. They'd been right, but he hadn't found it in him to give up any of the positions he'd taken on. Perhaps he should walk away from Caia in case she came to mean a lot to him, or she started to expect something more, especially with McKenzie in her life. That could set her up to be hurt, which was the last thing he wanted. Nor did he want to be hurt.

Caia turned to him. 'Lockie, if you're having second thoughts going out for a meal with me, then for goodness sake, say so now. The last thing I want is to sit at a table, picking at my food and wondering what's going on.'

If ever there was a reason to get to know her more, that was it. She was blunt, not simpering and trying to score points as other women did. His family's background of well-regarded medical specialists tended to attract women who wanted more than a three-bedroom, one-bath home and lifestyle. He'd become impervious to women over the years, believing he wasn't made for serious relationships after what happened with Marg. Nor did he ever want to be hurt so much again. If only it was easy falling in love with a woman who'd understand him and his needs and be with him forever. Seemed not in his case.

Click. Caia had undone her seatbelt. 'That's it. I'm done. See you tomorrow.'

He caught her hand. 'Caia, wait. I'm really sorry. I didn't mean to be remote. I want to spend time with you over dinner having nothing to do with work.'

'Then what's going on?' She wasn't backing down in a hurry. 'Thought we were going to talk about work, odd though that seems.'

He'd ignore that barb. 'I was overthinking things. I do that sometimes.'

'What were you thinking about?'

Of course she'd ask. 'Us. Me. Family. I have a very busy life and apart from golf, I don't get out much for enjoyment. When Izzy told us to go enjoy ourselves, it struck me how much I wanted to do exactly that, put work behind me and be social.' That didn't sound very inspiring. Caia would still get out of the car and go back inside her friend's house to be with her daughter.

'You're not a social man?'

'Depends how you look at it. I love getting out with friends and family whenever possible, but I'm involved in heavy workloads with the practise and the GP association board, so it's not as often as I'd like. Don't feel sorry for me. I chose this life, but there are drawbacks.' He started the car in the hope that Caia was still on for dinner. She didn't tell him to stop, so he made the most of the opportunity to head to the restaurant where he'd booked a table.

Instead she said, 'When McKenzie was so ill, I had very little time for anything but work, and even that was a struggle. As for anything else, I rarely got the vacuum cleaner out of the cupboard, let alone turned it on.'

'That's why I have a housekeeper.' He doubted Caia could afford one. 'I'm not trying to sound arrogant. It's only that having someone tidy up my home takes one pressure off my shoulders.'

'Believe me, if I had the money, I'd get one.' She faced him again. 'It is what it is. I put everything into looking after McKenzie, which includes a roof over our heads.'

'Are you renting?'

'No, I bought a small property three years ago, before she became ill. It needs work on it, which I'll eventually get done.'

'Go you.' He did have it easy in that respect. Sure, he'd had to save for the deposit on his house and would be paying off the mortgage for some time to come, but his university fees and medical school costs had been paid for by the family trust fund. No one in his family got everything on a plate, but they did get the basics to get started.

Not even Harry once he was back on his feet and looking forward to a bright future.

Harry had got an after school job at a hospital laboratory and spent the first weeks overcoming nausea brought on by testing blood samples. Now as a qualified pathologist specializing in haematology, he dealt with blood samples regularly and never thought twice about it.

'You're not the only doctor in your family, are you? When McKenzie was diagnosed with leukaemia, I looked up the pathologists and saw Harry Roberts's name on the list. He has an excellent reputation. Not that he saw McKenzie, but I confess that when I learned who was in the general practise where I was applying for the midwife position, I wondered if there was any connection and looked you up.'

'So you know our father was a cardiologist, and my uncles are both surgeons. Mum was a GP and following her career led me to choosing the same field. It was so intriguing to me. They're all retired now, but yes, medicine runs in the family.'

'Did you ever want to do something different?' Caia asked.

'When I was a young teenager, I thought being a high court judge would be interesting, wearing a wig and a black robe and handing down sentences to people who'd done heinous crimes. But when it came to making up my mind and deciding on the subjects to take at college, going the medical way was a no-brainer. It was the right fit. Chemistry came naturally, as did maths and biology. My parents never tried to push either me or Harry that way, said we had to make up our own minds, and if being a truckie appealed then go for it. But I couldn't deny the draw to medicine. It must run in the veins.' Hell, when was the last time he'd talked so much about himself? Time to shut up. 'Mum was a GP too. Really no getting away from it.' *Thought you were going to shut your mouth.*

'It's special having that link with your family.' Sadness resonated in her words. She hadn't had family sticking by her.

There wasn't a lot he could do or say about that without making her sadder, so he moved on. 'I hope you like seafood, as we're going to The Hook. I didn't think to check with you. They do a superb ribeye steak for people who don't eat fish.' She really did unnerve him.

'I love seafood, so you can relax.'

How did she know he was uptight? Because he was gripping the steering wheel too hard? 'You don't miss much.'

'That's because I'm a mother. Before then, you could've rubbed mud pie in my face and I wouldn't have noticed.'

'As if I'm going to believe that.' Thankfully the restaurant came into sight. Now he could get on with dinner and talking in a more open space, not having to breathe Caia's scent and feel her heat. 'Here we go.' Hopefully he'd be able to keep control over his tongue. Nothing to do with tasting Caia. All about not talking too much. But tasting Caia—now, that would be a treat. Dessert, maybe?

Sitting at the table in a quiet corner of the busy restaurant, Caia rolled her shoulders. The tightness in her muscles had been growing from the moment she heard Lockie talking to McKenzie. Not because she hadn't wanted him to meet her daughter, but she always got wary when a man turned up in her life. It didn't happen often, but there'd be a barrage of questions about Lockie tomorrow. Was he nice? Did he like her? Where did they go? Usually she blew off the questions with quick answers and distracted McKenzie with a game or something to eat. But somehow she didn't think it was going to be quite so easy this time. For one reason, Lockie had taken the time to acknowledge McKenzie and answer her questions. For another, Caia doubted this would be the only time her daughter would be seeing him. She wasn't thinking of the occasional times at night when she'd be overseeing a birth and McKenzie would be with her, snuggled up in a sleeping bag in a room next to the birthing unit, but at home, where work would have nothing to do with his visiting. She might be getting ahead of herself, but that's what kept her out of trouble.

As she watched him settle comfortably opposite her, a rush of adrenaline hit her. He was so good-looking it was all but impossible to focus on anything else. He might as well have taken her to a drive-through and bought burgers for all she cared. Dragging her gaze away, she looked around and changed her mind about burgers. 'This looks classy.' What would she know about classy? Very little, but no reason not to learn some more.

Lockie grinned. 'Glad you like it. A friend from my college days owns it. He's cooked in restaurants in Britain and Europe and knows what he's doing. Has awards to prove it too.'

'Would that be the chef heading this way?' She'd spied a guy in whites coming out from behind reception and looking around until his gaze landed on Lockie.

Twisting around, Lockie nodded. 'That's him.' He stood up. 'Callum, good to see you, mate.'

'Back at you.' They shared a man hug. Then Callum stepped back. 'Going to introduce me?'

'Caia, this is Callum De Bois. Callum, meet Caia Johnstone.'

Caia stood up and found her hand being engulfed in Callum's. 'Good to meet you,' she said.

'Same,' Callum said with a wide smile. 'Known

this blighter long? Or should I be filling you in on some of his habits?'

'Let's give him until after dessert before I go looking for answers about him.'

Both men laughed. Callum slapped Lockie on the back. 'You won't get time to eat much with all you've got to tell.'

'There's always the shortened version.'

Caia sat down, and Lockie followed suit. 'What would you recommend for mains, Callum?' she asked.

'The baked whole blue cod. It's from Foveaux Strait, caught yesterday.'

'My mouth's already watering. I don't need to read the menu.'

'You don't want to know what the cod comes with?'

'I'm sure it will be a perfect match, whatever you've prepared.'

'She's quite the charmer, isn't she?' Callum was grinning at Lockie as though there was a secret between them.

Lockie laughed, and there was a hint of surprise in his gaze. 'So it seems.'

'I'll get Regan to bring you over a glass of champagne to go with the cod,' Callum told her. 'Lockie, what would you like to drink?'

'The same, thanks. Caia, are you okay with champagne, or would you like something else?

Don't be reticent about saying what you like. Callum can take it.'

She wasn't an expert on wines, but champagne would be her pick any day of the week. 'I'm happy with champagne.'

'Sorted,' Callum said. 'Now, Lockie, what do you want to eat?'

'I haven't had time to look at the menu, man.' He picked one up and then dropped it. 'Damn it, what am I doing? The cod sounds delicious.'

'That was easy.' Callum collected the menus. 'I'll tell Regan what you want and to bring your drinks. Have a great night.' Then he was gone, pausing briefly here and there to say a word to other diners as he made his way through the room.

'He certainly knows how to keep his diners happy,' Caia said.

'He's always been like that, no matter what he's doing. Even at college, when he was injured badly enough not to continue his fledgling rugby career, he bounced back with a smile and utter confidence he could do well at anything he chose. Though sometimes he hid behind that enormous smile, keeping all but his closest friends at arm's length.'

'Sounds impressive.' She'd tended to go quiet around others at school when they asked questions about her family or why she didn't invite them to her house. Meeting her mother when she was in a depressed state was not on the cards any time for Caia. Easier to take the questions than deal with her mother trying to show her daughter's friends how wonderful mum was.

'Very,' Lockie agreed. 'A lot of people are, getting on with their day-to-day lives without making a big deal of it.' He was watching her as if referring to her.

'No one dodges all the bullets all the time,' she agreed. Not even her lovely wee girl. Life could be unfair, and the only way forward was to get up and keep going.

'You'd know all about that with McKenzie.'

Talk about being blunt. 'Yes, I do.' That's all she was saying. She didn't want Lockie feeling sorry for her. 'What bullets have you dealt with?' That'd change the subject in a hurry, unless Lockie felt like telling her more about himself, and she doubted he would. Not here over a special dinner anyway.

'Two glasses of champagne from the chef.' Regan placed one in front of her. 'Enjoy.'

'I will, thank you very much.' When Lockie picked up his, she tapped hers against it and said, 'Here's to a lovely night. Thank you for asking me out. It's kind of special.' For her, anyway.

'Glad you think that way. I understand why you wondered if we should go out together because of work, but I just wanted to get to know you a little and show that we are a great team at the practise with everyone watching out for each other.'

'I admit I worry that we might not get along very well, so thank you for asking me out. I need this job big time.'

'You're not supposed to tell your boss that.' Lockie grinned. Then he became serious. 'We all got that message during your interview, but it wasn't the reason you got the position. You come highly recommended, and from what I've seen so far, I understand why. So sit back, enjoy dinner, and forget all about work for a while.'

'You said discussing how my week was going was the reason to get together.'

'If you have any concerns about anything, then yes, I meant it. But first know that everyone's happy with how you're handling it all.'

That was a relief, even though she doubted she'd messed up. 'Then I'll enjoy dinner.'

'Good.' He sipped his champagne. 'That's superb.'

'I agree, though I'm no connoisseur.'

'You don't have to be. If you enjoy it, that's what counts.'

Not according to the last man she'd gone out with. Which was why she'd dumped him on the second date. That and his opinion children should be seen and not heard. 'Have you got any nieces or nephews?'

Lockie blinked at the change of subject. 'Not

one. Harry's never taken time out from work to have some fun. It's like he feels he owes everyone for being there when he was so ill. And pathology has to be one of the longest degrees in terms of years to obtain. He says he'll get around to finding the ideal woman in the next little while. That's if he can pull his head away from the microscope long enough.'

'Children would make him do that.' She wasn't asking where Lockie stood on the subject of having children. It had nothing to do with their date.

'So Mum keeps telling us. She can't wait to have grandchildren to fuss over. We're both tired of the fussing,' he added with a wry smile.

Missing out on that had made her feel unloved growing up, hence overdoing it with McKenzie, though she tried not to spoil her rotten. Hard not to when she'd nearly lost her to leukaemia. 'Families, eh?' How different they could be.

'How long have you and Izzy been mates?' Lockie had a habit of flicking from one subject to another whenever he wanted.

She couldn't complain. Getting away from talking about families suited her. 'Since we met at high school.' Izzy had accepted her for who she was, the most wonderful gift she'd ever had at that point in her life.

The waiter arrived bearing plates of delicious-looking food. 'Here you go, folks. Enjoy.'

Caia sighed with pleasure. 'This smells wonderful.'

'You haven't tasted it.' Lockie laughed.

She was drooling. 'I don't get to enjoy something so special very often.' How was that for honesty? No, if she was really honest, she'd say she'd almost never had anything like this.

'Then we'd better get along well so you can have some more delicious experiences.' Lockie picked up his glass. 'To a great dinner and more to come.'

Hesitating over picking up her glass to return the gesture, she wondered if that was what she wanted in the long run. To get to know Lockie and let him into her life seemed exciting, but it also worried her that once again, she'd be let down. If that happened, then McKenzie would also be let down, and she wouldn't allow that.

'Caia?'

To hell with it. As Izzy said, she worried far too much. Lifting her glass, she gave his a hearty tap. 'Bring it on.'

They sipped champagne, and she smiled. It was so good. As was the company. And by the looks of it, her meal. Actually, the company was way better than good. Lockie was phenomenal. She could sit here for hours watching him enjoy his meal, but then she'd miss out on appreciating hers. 'Thanks again for inviting me out,

Lockie.' He'd start thinking she was grovelling if she didn't shut up soon.

'I'm just glad you agreed to come out with me. Now let's eat before everything gets cold.'

Good idea. She gave him the thumbs-up and picked up a fork. Time to sit back and make the most of this with one very sexy gentleman.

'How was your meal?' Callum asked as Lockie pocketed his bank card.

Caia stepped forward. 'Superb, Callum. I really enjoyed it.'

'Seems she's easy to please,' Lockie quipped.

Caia's face dropped. Then the smile returned. 'I'm not someone who goes to restaurants often, but I know good food when I have it, and that meal was the best ever.' She was now looking at him and not Callum.

'You're bang-on, girlfriend.' What did he say? One glass of champagne and his tongue had got away on him. Nothing to do with the bubbles, and all because Caia was drop-dead gorgeous. 'I mean, my friend.'

Caia looked stunned.

Callum laughed. 'Get out of here. Seems you two have some things to sort out.'

Good idea. He helped Caia into her jacket before taking her elbow to lead her out to the car, where the winter chill hit hard. She was shivering under his hand. Because of the cold or because he was holding her, he didn't know. 'Sorry about that. I don't know what came over me.'

Pulling free, she turned to face him directly. 'You're confusing me. I know I'm not your girlfriend, so why call me that?' Her eyes bored into him as she waited for an answer.

Which he didn't have. Other than she'd turned him inside out with longing for her sexy body crushed against his as they made out. Not an answer he was ready to give. 'We've had a wonderful night, and I'm relaxed.' Too relaxed, it seemed. 'I truly have enjoyed myself. I hope you feel the same.' She had him on the back foot. Never had he tried so hard to keep a woman onside. But this particular one was changing how he felt about getting to know her more. He wanted to get even closer. She wasn't one he was in a hurry to have a short fling with and then go his own way without regrets.

Those intense eyes remained fixed on him, but her expression had softened, and that tempting mouth was curving upward. 'I do. I couldn't have asked for a better time.'

That smile was growing, sexy and tantalising as it could possibly be. Without thinking, he hauled her into his arms and covered her smile with his mouth. She tasted as good as she looked. Curvy and sexy. He held her tight, feeling her breasts pressed against his chest, her thighs pushing against his, setting him alight with need as her arms surrounded him and held him close. Arousing his sex, hardening him. With his tongue, he delved deeper into her mouth, wanting to taste and feel her. It wasn't enough. Nowhere near it. He wanted all of her. Wanted to make love, to know that sublime body for top to toe, to feel her satin-like skin under his fingertips, to press into her heat.

Voices reached him from the restaurant entrance, cutting through the haze blurring his mind.

He straightened, setting Caia back on her feet but still holding her. The last thing he wanted was to let her go. 'Let's get out of here.'

She stepped away from him, her fingers on her lips. Glancing up at him, she nodded slowly. Too slowly for his liking. 'I agree.'

That had to be all right, didn't it? Yet there was a *but* in her voice, in her stance. Had he come on too fast? 'But?'

'I think I should go pick up McKenzie now.' She bit down on her bottom lip.

'Fair enough.' It was nowhere near fair, but he wasn't one to push a woman into doing something she didn't want. He opened the car door, ignoring the thumping going on in his chest. So this was what disappointment felt like? Serious disappointment when a woman turned him down? Not any woman. Caia.

She placed her hand on his arm. 'I'm sorry, Lockie. I'm not used to this.'

This? 'As in what?'

'I don't date very often, and even when I do, I tend to take my time getting to know the man before anything else happens.'

Her words struck him deeply. The hurt she'd experienced from her ex was written all over her face and in her crumpled posture. He reached over and pulled her into the gentlest hug he could manage while his body was crying out for more. She'd wound him tighter than ever. 'It's okay, Caia. I can handle it, and I'd like to get to know you better, too.' He kissed the top of her head. He had to. There was no other option. She had made her decision. There were two involved when it came to having sex, not one. 'Let's go back to your friend's so you can collect your girl.'

Pulling away, she looked up at him with troubled eyes. 'Why are you being so nice?'

'I'm not into deliberately hurting someone.' That man who'd hurt her better hope he never bumped into him, because there would be trouble.

With a trembling hand, she touched his cheek. 'You're special.' Then she turned, got into the car and closed the door. The evening was over. As long as that was all that was over, he'd handle it.

Caia couldn't talk on the way back to Izzy's. Her mouth was dry, and there was a lump the size of a rock in the back of her throat making it difficult for air to get past. Once again, Lockie had proved how wonderful he was. Even better, not demanding she do as he expected. Not implying that she owed him for a wonderful dinner. He was so different he rattled her. She only wished she hadn't kissed him, and obviously turned him on, then pulled back. It wasn't fair on Lockie. Nor her because she really did want him. Not only physically but as someone important in her life.

So why had she pulled back? She'd finally met someone she was starting to see could be right for her. She'd got cold feet when she was so hot for him she'd believed she was going to combust. Right now her body was crying out to be held in Lockie's strong arms while he made love to her.

Except he'd want nothing more to do with her outside work. Like other men she'd turned down. They had hurried into this situation. First by going on a date so soon after she'd started working for the practise, then by kissing in the car park like there was no tomorrow. But some dates went that way, all or nothing. What felt right was right. She wanted it all but couldn't find it in her to say so. He'd turn her down anyway now that she'd backed off.

Went to show how much Garth had screwed with her thinking if she couldn't trust another man to give her a good time without hurting her. Garth had also left his unborn baby behind. Not once had he got in touch to find out if he had a son or a daughter or ask if he could meet him or her. That didn't make every other man she went out with into a monster. There were some great guys out there. Izzy had nailed one. Lockie might be one, which had a lot to do with why she'd accepted his invitation tonight. But she couldn't shake the habit of protecting herself so that she could look out for McKenzie as well as herself. No one was going to let her girl down, but if she didn't take some risks then McKenzie would never know what it was like to have a loving father, something she very much wanted her to experience.

Lockie pulled into Izzy's driveway and stopped. Turning to Caia, he looked her in the eye.

Her breath stuck in her throat. What was he going to say? She didn't want to hear how she'd let him down or that he didn't want her to work with him. 'I'm sorry,' she croaked.

'Don't be. You did what was right for you.'

She blinked at him. Finally drew air into her lungs. 'You're very understanding.'

'There's a way to go before I fully understand, but believe me when I say I'm not pushing you aside because you decided not to get any closer to me tonight.'

'But you are pushing me aside?' Sounded like that to her.

He shook his head. 'No, not at all.'

If he kept this up, she'd have tears streaming down her face, which would be downright embarrassing. 'It might be better for you if you did.' She wasn't used to a man being this open when it came to his emotions.

He straightened in his seat and picked up her hand. 'I can look out for myself. It's you I'm concerned about. But let's leave this conversation for now. You look whacked, and you've still got to go home with McKenzie. As for work, let's go for friendly co-workers. I don't want to be sniping with you or looking out for where you are so I can avoid you. Nor do I want to be watching out to make sure you're all right. We'd have Katie and Dave on our backs as quick as the kettle comes to the boil.' He gave her a soft smile.

Her heart melted a little. Lockie knew how to boost her confidence, something she only lacked when around men she was interested in. Not Lockie, she conceded. She hadn't felt unsure of how to get along with him until that moment when they pulled apart outside the restaurant and the old insecurities flooded her mind. She squeezed his hand before letting go to open the door. 'We have a deal. I'll see you tomorrow.' She got out and quickly headed to the house, unwilling to slow and look back for fear she'd rush back to his car and leap in, telling him to take her somewhere so they could make love. At the moment, her body was screaming to come to the boil herself and let go all over him.

Even after she'd rushed inside and banged the door shut behind her, she didn't hear Lockie drive off. He must have. He wouldn't be sitting there waiting for her to leave with McKenzie. She wouldn't know what to make of that if he was. Because if Lockie was still there, it probably meant he was looking out for her. Another thing she wasn't used to, and didn't need. But would like very much.

'Hey, Caia, you're back early. How did dinner go?' Izzy came along the hall.

Caia took one look at her friend and burst into tears. 'I messed up completely.' She'd been a total ass and knew she was going to regret it for a while to come. 'I let all my fears get in the way of having some fun.'

'Really? Dinner was a waste of time?'

'You know what I mean.' Izzy understood her too well. 'Dinner was stupendous. So was the company.'

'Then roll with that and stop overthinking everything. You obviously had a good time, so don't let your thoughts get in the way of you being happy. Who knows what's ahead?'

Would she get another chance with Lockie? If she did, she wouldn't make the same mistake. Would she? No. Probably. Hopefully not.

CHAPTER FIVE

LOCKIE STARED AT the screen before him, trying to concentrate on patient notes and not Caia. The fact was, she hadn't left his mind all weekend. Whenever he did fall asleep, she was there, taunting him with questions about what had made her so wary. If only he could walk up to her and ask directly what had gone on that put her so on edge with him.

But it wouldn't work. He mightn't know Caia well, but he understood that she'd back away and head for the hills rather than answer him. She was a battler if the few comments she'd made about looking out for McKenzie were correct, and she'd be fierce about keeping an eye out for herself too even if only to place her daughter out of harm's way.

Running his fingers through his thick hair, he groaned. Of all the women he'd known over the years, not one had fascinated him nearly as much as Caia. Nor had any of them filled him with a deep need to give all he could physically. Also to look out for her in other ways.

It was happening too fast, too soon. Their dinner date hadn't slowed a thing. Instead it hyped up the ante despite him feeling unready to take chances with love again. This wasn't only about satisfying his sexual needs. This was about Caia, the woman behind the tantalising body. The woman with demons in her approach to him. She'd been badly hurt, and he wanted to make her feel safe with him. But he wasn't sure he was ready for that either as it would expose his own fears and could well make things worse for her. He so wanted to be able to move past Marg and the regrets she'd caused, but could he?

Too often he'd been told he was more focused on work and his own needs than anyone else's, and that he had to make a choice between all the work he did and devoting time to that special person in his life. In other words, he was self-centred. He was afraid to try again, not wanting to feel the pain of losing someone he'd entrusted with his heart. The guilt he'd known over his wife's suicide might have lessened over the years, but he was still flummoxed about how he hadn't seen it coming. Nor had her parents, who'd been close to Marg, having dealt with her first attempt when she was fifteen—something else Marg never told him. Her parents still didn't recognise the signs. If the light of his life could do that, then he wasn't prepared to take a chance on letting someone else into his heart. But no denying Caia was tapping at his door a little too easily for his liking. She was waking him up, exciting him and filling him with hope for the future.

Along came Caia, and suddenly he was all out of excuses to stay clear of a relationship. On Friday night, she'd given him a doozy by stepping back. Especially when she'd kissed him like there was no stopping her. Did that mean she wasn't ready for a new relationship either? Most likely.

A fling wouldn't cut it. Not when they were both vulnerable. Not when Caia had a daughter to put first. He wouldn't want to hurt McKenzie either, he reminded himself, in case he needed another excuse to step away before they became more entangled.

But having felt off-centre since that very first time he saw Caia meant perhaps these feelings weren't quite as strange as he thought. Maybe there was a connection between them that neither had any control over. He'd often heard people say they'd fallen for the person of their heart in one look. He never really believed it to be that easy to hand over *his* heart. Not after Marg. But was he falling for Caia little by little? It hadn't only been that time on the ward that he'd felt a pull towards her. It had happened again the day she came for her interview. And last week when she arrived at work for the first time.

'Knock, knock, can I come in?' the receptionist asked.

Lockie spun around on his chair. 'Why ask? You usually barge right on in like it's your office.'

'Because I've been talking to you for at least two minutes, and you haven't heard a word.' Annie laughed. 'Something on your mind that's got nothing to do with work?'

Someone, not something. 'I was reading some lab results that don't add up to what I'd been expecting.'

Annie's eyes widened as she glanced at his screen. 'Really?'

Oh, great. The screen was showing his appointments for the morning, nothing from the lab. Unable to come up with a believable explanation, he shrugged. 'Caught. What can I do for you?'

'Everyone's waiting for you.' She paused. When he didn't react, she said almost condescendingly, 'Monday morning…? Staff meeting?'

Ouch. He stood up too fast, causing his head to spin. 'Coming.'

A voice he'd recognise even if he was asleep reached him from along the hall, sounding as tired as he felt. Had he been in Caia's head as much as she'd been in his? Part of him hoped so, while the reasonable side of his brain felt unkind because that'd mean she'd be tired before she'd even started work for the week. Whether she'd slept well or not, he hadn't, which only underlined how much she was affecting him.

Stepping into the staffroom, he ignored the grins coming his way. What did they know about his state of mind? 'Morning, everyone. Sorry to keep you waiting.'

Caia nodded at a mug of coffee on the table. 'Your caffeine fix.' Dark shadows lay beneath her dimmed eyes.

Which made him feel a little guilty. She needed her sleep as much as anyone, especially since she was a single mother as well as having to come to work. 'Thanks.'

He picked up the mug, took a mouthful and tried to get on with the day, Caia or no Caia to screw with his brain.

Plonking her butt on the chair at her desk, Caia dropped her head in her hands. *Lockie, Lockie, Lockie. What are you doing to me?*

Just hearing him talk, that deep voice knocked aside all intentions of being totally focused on work and nothing else. What to do? But getting on with the job, not veering off to dreams about what it would be like to have a wonderful man in her life permanently, was the only option.

'You all right, Caia?' Katie strode into the room looking concerned. 'You look whacked.'

Jerking upright, Caia dug for a smile. 'I'm

fine.' Okay, that wasn't going to work. 'Didn't get a lot of sleep last night, that's all.'

Katie eyed her up and down. 'You're not worried about something? The job?'

'Not at all. I'm loving it.'

Katie smiled. 'Glad to hear it.' She sat down and crossed her legs. 'Just remember, if there's anything you need or want to know, don't hesitate to ask me.'

That'd be easier than knocking on Lockie's door. 'I'll do that.'

'The list of patients waiting to meet you is already growing. More than the ones we mentioned at your interview. Seems word's got out that we've taken on a midwife, and women want to come on board ASAP.'

'That's great.' It was why she was here and what made her happy. Babies and more babies. Happy mums and dads.

'Don't overdo it and get exhausted too fast,' Katie warned.

'No, Boss.' She smiled. 'I'll behave, I promise.'

'That's what I like to hear.' Katie got to her feet. 'I'd better get cracking. The waiting room's filling up fast.'

Caia looked at her screen to see when her first patient was booked in. Half an hour away. After opening the file, she read notes from the woman's previous midwife.

Jillian Gilmour, DOB 16-05-2000. Third pregnancy, nearing end of second trimester. No difficulties with first and second, none so far with this one. I suggested she try a vegetarian diet as she's overweight for this stage in her pregnancy, but she refuses. Says she lost any weight gained after giving birth to her two sons.

Caia sat back in her chair and reread the notes. Why had Jillian changed her midwife? Could it have something to do with the unusual dietary advice? That was definitely a little odd. The notes came from a midwifery clinic further north of the city. Judging by Jillian's address, she had a way to travel to get here which said she wasn't happy with where she had been attending. 'Probably reading too much into this,' Caia admitted.

Fingers crossed her patient wouldn't be tetchy and start grizzling about her previous midwife, because she'd be shut down fast. She didn't do talking about other midwives. It wasn't on. In the years since she'd qualified and begun practising, she'd had to deal with only one instance where another midwife had taken a patient off her, and that had been because the woman was related to the midwife. Caia felt it wasn't right for the midwife to look after a relative, or even allowable, but she'd kept her mouth shut and left it up to other, more qualified people to resolve the matter. In the end, the pregnant woman had changed midwives yet again, opting for one working with her relative she'd gone to, and everyone was happy.

The phone on her desk buzzed. 'Your first patient's here early.'

'I'll be along in a minute.' A buzz filled her. Already she felt she belonged here. Working in a medical centre where other people came for more than midwifery was interesting, even though she didn't have anything to do with them. It also wasn't as lonely as working either as a solo midwife or in a midwifery clinic where there wasn't always a lot going on. Had she found her niche? As long as she and Lockie didn't get into a mess, then all would be good. This could be her forever job.

'Jillian?' A pregnant woman looked up. 'I'm Caia Johnstone, the clinic's midwife.'

A well-dressed, not very overweight woman stood up with her hand on her lower back. 'Hello, Caia. I'm glad to meet you.'

'Come through to my room.' She led the way, giving Jillian a once over as they went. 'Are you uncomfortable somewhere?' The way Jillian was pressing against her lower back suggested she had some aches.

'That's why I made the appointment. I'm getting twitches in my back that I didn't have with my other pregnancies. I hope nothing's going wrong.'

'Have you done any heavy lifting or moving too fast?' She indicated the door into her room. 'Through here.'

Jillian slipped past her and sat down. 'I've been shifting sacks of chook feed as my husband's away for work. We've got a lifestyle block with free-range hens on the edge of the city,' she explained. 'He's not usually away, but his company had an emergency and asked him to go down to Wellington to sort it.'

Closing the door, Caia made for her chair. 'You know what I'm going to say about lifting those sacks, don't you?' At least Jillian hadn't hesitated about telling her what she'd been doing.

'I do, and you're quite right, but I wasn't going to hide the truth in case I have caused trouble for baby. He comes before my pride.' Her smile was woeful. 'Hauling around bags of meal and full cans of water is normally part of my routine day. Since I've had no indications of not being up to speed, it never occurred to me not to carry on as usual.'

'I'm not going to give you a speech. I'll only say that from now on, you need to be more careful.'

'I hear you.' She blinked as though tears weren't far away. 'It's only that I hate feeling incapacitated. Especially when I'm healthy. My previous midwife kept insisting I go on a vegetarian diet to keep my weight in check, but I don't believe I'm overweight. What do you think?'

Here they went, the problem she'd hoped to avoid. 'You should stick with what you're used to unless you're eating loads of unhealthy or fried foods. A complete change in your diet at this stage could make you more tired as your body adjusts. Hop on the scale so I can note your weight.'

Jillian smiled down at the reading. 'Same as last time. I never put on a lot of weight during my previous pregnancies, and what I did gain disappeared soon after the births.'

'Good. I'll check your blood pressure and heart rate before doing an internal to make sure everything's ticking along as it should.' There was still the ache in Jillian's back to discuss.

After returning to the chair, her patient held her arm out for the BP cuff. 'Where did you work before coming here?'

'Parnell. I covered for a midwife on maternity leave.' Would she ever have another baby and take her own maternity leave? That particular question had started popping up in her mind lately, something she'd never considered before. She had McKenzie and hadn't felt the need to have another child. She'd been so lucky that McKenzie survived, she was more than happy not have another child. Yet here she was wondering about it. Silly when her hands were full with her career and McKenzie. 'BP's normal. You're in good shape. Up on the bed for the internal.' No need to spell out the procedure. Jillian would have it down pat.

Jillian sprawled on her back and lifted her buttocks to haul her jeans down to her ankles.

Gloves on, Caia knelt at the end of the bed. 'Any pain since your last check-up? Any tightness in your lower abdomen?'

'No. Only discomfort when baby starts kicking his football around my belly.'

'Football, eh?'

'My other two are already mad about the game. I think my husband's looking for us to have a whole team.'

'That'd be interesting, not to say exhausting on all fronts.'

'It's all right. He went off the idea when I said he'd have to take over the cooking and housework because I'd be too exhausted to cope.'

The room fell quiet as Caia slipped the speculum inside Jillian's vagina to check the cervix size, then the position of the fetus. 'Noah's in a good place, and everything is as it should be.'

Jillian expelled a loud sigh. 'That's a relief. I always worry in case something goes wrong.'

Snapping off her gloves, Caia smiled at her. 'That's normal. Most women say pretty much the same thing.' Caia filled in the notes on screen, then turned to face Jillian. 'About your backache.'

She grimaced. 'Yes?'

'Are you taking anything for it?'

'No.'

'I'm going to prescribe paracetamol to be taken twice a day. You must not lift heavy weights, which is likely the cause. If the ache gets worse or doesn't go away within the next week, then I want to see you again.' She could do firm when necessary. 'Understand?'

'Yes, I do. And no, I won't lift anything heavier than a loaf of bread until after Noah arrives.'

'Good. I'm looking forward to working with you until your wee man makes his appearance.'

'I'm glad to have changed to you. You've made me feel quite relaxed, whereas I was starting to get a bit wound up with my last midwife.'

Not going there. 'Pleased I could help.' She opened the door and followed Jillian out to reception before heading to the break room for a much-needed caffeine fix. She was pleased with how that had gone. It was always a bit of a wait-and-see moment when meeting a patient for the first time. She had to get along with the mother or it could be a fiasco. Not that she'd ever really had problems with any patient over the years she'd been doing this, but being cautious wasn't a bad habit. It kept her on her toes and prevented her from getting blasé about the job. As if she ever would.

* * *

'How's your morning going?' Lockie asked when Caia walked into the break room. She looked just as tantalising in pants and a floral blouse as she had in that sexy red pantsuit she'd worn to dinner on Friday. Why hadn't they put in the contract that she had to wear track pants and a hoodie when at work? Except she'd no doubt make those look sexy too. Damn it. This wasn't going quite as well as he'd hoped.

'Not bad,' she replied. 'Keeping busy and out of trouble.'

'That's what we like to hear,' Dave acknowledged with a grin. 'Help yourself to a biscuit. Charlotte, my wife, has been cooking up a storm.'

'They look yummy.' She picked up an afghan and bit into it, rolling her eyes as she chewed.

'Now we know how to keep her quiet,' Lockie said. Not that she was overly talkative, sometimes too quiet for his liking. Especially when he was trying to find out more about what made her tick. 'How was McKenzie this morning? Happy to go to school?' He was talking too much if the surprise on Dave's face was anything to go by. Tough. This was how he ran whenever Caia was around, and they'd all better get used to it. As he had to, he admitted to himself.

'Once I put peanut butter on her sandwich and not honey as intended, she was fine.' The loving grin lifting her face made him envious of her daughter.

He'd like nothing more than to be on the receiving end of a few of those. 'Easily pleased. Make the most of it. I'm sure it will get trickier as she gets older.'

'Bang-on,' Dave agreed. 'My boys wouldn't be seen dead with a homemade sandwich at school. Though they do take the biscuits their mother bakes for them as their friends get all jealous.'

'Parenthood, eh?' No winning by the sounds of it. Maybe it wasn't such a bad idea to stay away from having kids. No, he didn't believe that in any way. Kids were delightful even if a handful. He'd love a couple of little ones running around him, a boy and a daughter with hectic red hair like her mother's. His glance slid to Caia. His mug hit the table, and coffee splashed over his hand. What the hell was he thinking? He and Marg had never got around to discussing when they'd start a family, leaving that for when they both felt they had the time. He'd wanted to wait until he'd qualified, while Marg hadn't said when, just sometime. But he had always wanted a family. And now? He still wasn't ready. First he had to find the special woman to share his life and then his children with.

'I do have a question,' Caia said as she stared at the mess on the table.

Don't ask me why I can picture my daughter

with your hair colouring. He grabbed a cloth to wipe up the coffee.

'What's that?' Dave asked.

'Not all my patients belong to the general practice and only come to the midwifery clinic. If I get a patient here who I think needs instant attention from a doctor and they're not a patient of this clinic, do I still come ask one of you to see her?'

He could answer that without getting in a fix over red hair. 'Talk to Val first, and she'll arrange for one of us to see the woman. It'll depend on who's free at the time. If the patient insists on going to her doctor and you can't change her mind, then phone ahead and tell them what's going on.'

Caia nodded. 'I figured that'd be the answer, but I like to be sure.'

No surprise. That was one thing he'd worked out about Caia right from the get-go. Rinsing his mug, he decided to cut his break short and go find some air without citrus to breathe. Or maybe his next patient would be waiting and give him something else to focus on. So much for thinking he could work alongside Caia without any difficulty. Having kissed her and been kissed in return, he felt he was walking a tightrope over a deep canyon. Fall and he was screwed. Stay on the rope and he'd be constantly balancing himself to stay upright. Put that way, he might as well get off the rope and invest all he had in finding out where this was going. Caia wouldn't mess around. She'd either be with him or tell him she wasn't interested in having another date and furthering where that kiss had been heading before she pulled back.

'Hi, Lockie. Am I glad to see you.' Jonno Murphy stood up as he entered the waiting room.

'Come though.' Nothing like keeping ahead of the schedule, and having someone to focus on who didn't distract him other than in medical terms. 'How have you been?' Silly question. He knew all about Jonno's aches and pains as he'd been treating him for arthritis for a long time, and until Jonno followed up on suggestions for relief nothing was going to change. Hauling on a smile, he nodded to Jonno take a seat by the desk.

'A lot better since you put me on those anti-depressants.'

So he was taking those tablets. It was a start. 'Glad they're working.' He closed the door to his room behind Jonno and took a seat at his desk. 'You look more relaxed than last time I saw you. Have you been seeing a counsellor?' Always a tricky one as many people didn't believe they needed to bare their souls to a stranger.

'I have, and she's helped me a lot.'

'I'm pleased.' Should he see one and solve his dilemma about getting into a relationship again? During the horrific first year after Marg committed suicide, he'd spent many hours having counselling, trying to get his head around why she'd do something so horrific. She had everything going for her as a lawyer and often talked about setting up her own practise. The guilt he'd known because he hadn't recognised she wasn't coping with life as well as he'd believed had been immense, but so too had been the pain of losing the woman he'd loved with all his being.

But now? What did he truly want for the future? Until Caia arrived in his life, he hadn't even thought about it other than as a passing moment of indecision. Now he thought about her in numerous ways.

Jonno coughed as though trying to get his attention.

'Sorry, Jonno. Slip your sleeve up and I'll take your BP.' It'd been marginally raised last visit. 'We'll keep the antidepressant dosage the same for now since it's working. Is that all right with you?'

'Whatever you say. I feel a lot better and don't want to go backwards because I stopped taking them too soon.'

'Decision made. Your blood pressure's normal. Seems like you're improving.'

He filled in the prescription, and they discussed Jonno getting outdoors more since he sat at a desk all day for work. 'I'll see you again in three months.' Opening the door, he said, 'Carry on the good work.'

A quirky laugh that warmed his blood—and

his heart—came from the reception area. Definitely going to have to spend more time with that woman and calm the unprecedented upheaval going on in his head 24/7.

CHAPTER SIX

THE FOLLOWING FRIDAY afternoon, Caia was at home early. She'd seen several patients over the day and was not needed anywhere else which suited her fine. The number of patients was growing slowly so she had no worries about making the most of the free time. Katie suggested she get away while she could with the proviso that she was available if required. That was a no-brainer. She was always available for patients in difficulty, so she'd happily tidied up her rooms and gone to collect McKenzie.

Two weeks finished and she'd loved every moment, including the edgy moments around Lockie. He tipped her sideways far too easily when it came to thinking if he could be more than a colleague, even more than a friend. The date had been awesome despite how she'd pulled the plug on continuing the kiss. Caution was her mentor, but she admitted that sometimes she probably took it too far. There was nothing wrong in having a good time with a decent man, even letting loose and getting her clothes off once in a while. It didn't mean she had to fall for the guy or want to spend lots of time with him.

'Can't wait until you have to explain to McKenzie when she's older why she can't just rock up to a hot dude and have her way with him,' Izzy commented with a laugh when Caia said the same to her over a glass of wine twenty minutes later.

'Are you saying I'm acting like a trollop?' she asked. She wasn't going to think about McKenzie becoming a teenager and ogling boys like there was nothing else worth looking at. That was a few years away. Unless she locked McKenzie up until she was thirty.

'Why not? It's about time you shucked off the doubts you harbour and let rip occasionally.' Izzy grinned, then turned serious. 'I mean it, Caia. I know Garth hurt you badly, but not all men are like him. You've got to take risks to get what you truly want. I think it's past time to start putting your toes in the dating water and seeing who's out there.'

'Lockie Roberts, for one.' He'd said there was no one deep and meaningful in his life, and she believed him. But then, she'd believed Garth when he'd said he loved her and was there for the long haul. She sighed. 'You're right. I am screwed up about romance because of Garth.' She tapped her glass to Izzy's. 'As of now, I let it go. He's history.' He had been for years, but whenever another man interested her, Garth somehow snuck back into her head to taunt her about the night he left her.

'You have to mean it, Caia.'

Locking eyes with her friend, she drew a deep breath. 'You know what? I do. It's been long enough, too long, to waste any more of my life on what might've been. It's time to get out and find what will be.' She took a big mouthful. 'Talk about getting serious.'

'You're often serious.' Izzy smiled. 'But I like that you're that way about this. I want to get to know Lockie since it's obvious he's the one responsible for your change of heart.'

Heart? Therein lay the problem. She didn't want it thrown under a bulldozer again. But she also wasn't keen on running solo forever. 'How about I put on a barbecue tonight and invite him to join us?'

'Brett will get the steak.'

It was a regular joke between them that Caia couldn't be trusted to buy good steak. 'You're on.' Suddenly she felt lighthearted and happy. She was getting a life. Whether a better one or not remained to be seen.

Lockie swung his club, sending the golf ball over the green.

'Not bad, old boy.' His mate, Terry, lined up his ball.

Not bad? 'It was a brilliant shot.' Not that he was bragging. Not much. His phone vibrated in his pocket. Tempted to ignore it as it was his day off from everything workwise, he found he couldn't. It could be anybody, even someone he was desperate to hear from…

Caia's name was on the screen. 'Hi. Have you got a problem with a patient?'

'Ahh, no. Sorry, I was ringing about something that has nothing to do with work.'

She was phoning him? Anticipation started firing up. 'And that would be?'

'Izzy, her husband, Brett, and the kids are coming around for a barbecue later. Would you like to join us?' The words rushed at him as though she was afraid she wouldn't get them all out.

'That'd be great,' he replied, not allowing himself time to overthink it. 'What can I bring?'

'Whatever you like to drink. We'll be starting about five as the kids need to be fed early.'

'No problem.' He'd drop by the supermarket for cheeses and dips to take along, as well as beer and wine. 'What does Brett drink?'

'Lager. But you don't have to get any. He'll bring his own.'

Terry was waiting in the golf cart. 'I've got to go. I'm at the golf course, but I'm looking forward to seeing you later.' He wasn't lying. They'd managed to keep the heat between them under control throughout the week, but it didn't mean he wasn't thinking about Caia all the time when nothing else distracted him. Now he was going to Caia's place for a meal with her and her friends. And three little girls. Very homely. He grinned. It didn't bother him one iota. Instead, it was exciting.

'What are you grinning about?' Terry asked. 'Got a new bit on the side lined up?'

Ouch. That hurt, even if there was some truth in the implication his relationships were only flings. Caia was either more than that or nothing at all. 'I'm going to a family barbecue later today.'

'And you're grinning like you've won the lotto? Who's going to be there to put that grin on your face?'

'Wouldn't you like to know?'

'That's why I'm asking.'

Lockie lined up the ball and sussed out the green ahead. 'Time to get this show back on track.'

'Good game, Terry,' Lockie conceded at the eighteenth hole. He hadn't been concentrating as much as usual, a certain red-haired woman intervening with his concentration at the worst possible moments. Like when he'd lined up the ball and was about to swing his club or make a delicate putt towards the hole. 'My shout.' It was part of their day on the course to follow up with a beer in the clubrooms.

'Of course it is.' Terry was wearing that annoying grin that said, *You lost, buddy.*

Caia's nerves were stretched to the limit. 'McKenzie, what are you doing with the peg basket?'

'Decorating the plants on the deck.'

Wonderful. But really, what did it matter? A few pegs here and there was less of a mess than the mud cakes she'd made last time Izzy's lot came for a meal. 'Don't clip any on the flowers, okay?'

'Yes, Mum.' A tired, *what do you take me for?* answer.

Caia managed a smile. She was the tired one around here. Nights of sleep interspersed with thoughts and visions of Lockie didn't make for restful hours. Nor did reliving that kiss. Now he'd be joining them tonight. As long as Izzy kept quiet on how she felt about Caia getting together with Lockie for more than a brief fling, then she'd handle the night. She had to. There was no alternative.

Toot, toot, toot. Izzy's tribe had arrived. 'Come on, McKenzie. Jessie and Jodie are here.'

'I'm busy.' She was lining up a peg, head to one side as though this had to be perfect. 'Do you think Lockie will like this?'

What? Where was her phone? She needed to call to tell him not to come. She couldn't have McKenzie getting too intense about him visiting.

No way. She'd get her little heart broken, and that was only happening over *her* dead body. No one was hurting McKenzie.

'Hey, you.' Brett wrapped an arm around her shoulders. 'What are you looking so serious about?'

'Was I? Sorry, must've been having a blonde moment.' Not sharing even though she could with Brett. He had her back as much as Izzy.

'Then smile, Blondie.' Izzy came up the steps with a bag of food and a bottle of wine.

Blondie was better than strawberry head. The tension backed off. Thankfully McKenzie had been diverted by the girls. She'd overreacted, but it was called self-protection. And daughter protection. Somehow she smiled. Easier than getting a lecture from Izzy or Brett. 'Lockie is coming.'

'Hence that look. You're already worrying about how things will go. Give it a break and relax.'

Brett glanced across at the girls now all pegging the shrubs. 'McKenzie can handle it. She's one tough cookie.'

True. Going though leukaemia and the treatment had done that for her. 'But—'

'But nothing. Life's not a one-way road with picnics along the way.' Brett gave her another hug. 'Now, did you get a new gas cylinder?'

That had been one of many things to do she'd

written on a list throughout the morning. 'Attached and ready to use.'

'Lockie's here,' McKenzie cried and raced off the deck, followed by the other two imps shouting, 'Lockie, Lockie.'

Suddenly Caia burst out laughing. 'Blimey. This is crazy.'

Her friends laughed too. 'You can say that again,' Brett commented. 'Who knows what's ahead, but you should enjoy what you can.'

'Seems I've missed out on a joke,' Lockie said from the deck as the girls raced around him in a circle, squealing like he'd brought them chocolate bars.

'Just as well,' Caia muttered, still relaxed even as her heartbeat lifted at the wonderful sight before her. 'Come in. Don't mind the girls. They'll get out of your way.'

'I like being the centre of attention.' Lockie grinned.

Brett stepped forward, hand out. 'Brett, Izzy's other half. Father of two of your admirers.'

Lockie shook his hand. 'That'll wear off, though maybe not until after I show them what's in my bag,' he said without looking in the children's direction.

Little Miss Big Ears stopped running and piped up, 'What did you get us?'

'Nothing you can have before dinner, okay?'

McKenzie pulled a face. 'Why?'

'Because I said so.'

'You're just like Mummy.'

Lockie nodded. 'Then we're on the same page.'

'What's that mean?'

'That you can't have your treat till later.'

McKenzie shook her head. 'What's the treat?'

'You're not finding out till later.' Lockie wasn't an easy target.

Caia smiled happily. He wasn't trying to get to her through her daughter. Unless that was why he was standing by what he believed would be her rules, but she didn't think so. Lockie did things the way he wanted and wasn't fazed by how other people perceived him. Hopefully he was as open and honest about everything that might affect her. Not that she could think of anything he might want from her as Garth had. 'Can I get you a drink?'

'I've brought beers.' He held out the bag he was carrying. 'Along with various dips and crackers, plus a bottle of wine I would've got something for dinner, but it sounded like you had that in hand.'

'Everything's sorted, nothing too glamorous.'

'Apart from the chocolate gateau I whipped up.' Izzy handed Caia a glass of wine. 'There you go. Get some of that into you and relax.'

Taking the glass, she couldn't help but smile. 'You're such a nag.' Nothing new there, and now that Lockie was here, Izzy would up the ante over the evening.

'Only way to get through to you.'

Lockie shook his head. 'Now I see where the girls get their cheeky banter from.'

Brett held out a beer. 'Come out on the deck, Lockie. These two can go on for hours.'

Even knowing Izzy was observing her, it was difficult for Caia to take her eyes off Lockie. She couldn't get enough of that amazing sight. Where was this heading? She really needed to know before she made a complete fool of herself.

'How about jumping right in?' Izzy was at her side, looking in the same direction.

'I don't know how to do that.'

'Judging by that stunned look on your face, I'd say you're about to learn real fast.' Izzy tapped her glass against Caia's. 'Come on. Let's join the guys and make the most of the time we're together.'

It turned out to be easier than Caia expected. Lockie fitted in with her friends as though he'd known them for ages. He and Brett got into a conversation about car racing that went on and on until she asked Brett to get the barbecue cranked up for the steak and sausages.

Lockie gave her a hand bringing out the salads and baked potatoes plus the condiments she'd prepared. 'This is fun. Thanks for asking me along.'

'Anytime.' Oops. Well, maybe if they continued to get along in such a relaxed manner. 'It's a simple way to be with my friends and not leave McKenzie out of the picture.'

His gaze tracked to the girls now dressing their dolls in pink costumes. 'I can't imagine her letting you get away with that.'

'You're right, she wouldn't. It's comes from her recovery after being so ill last year. She's tough and won't let people ignore her, nor put her down over anything. Especially kids her age.'

'Did the treatment knock her about badly?'

'Yes. Getting near the end she was extremely lethargic and unaware of anything going on around her. But she's making up for it now. I'm ever so grateful to whoever donated the bone marrow that saved her life. Being faced with losing her was the hardest thing I've ever had to do.'

Lockie wrapped an arm around her waist and drew her closer. 'I cannot begin to imagine what you went through.'

Except that wasn't true. The memories of Harry being so ill he couldn't lift his head off the pillow had never left completely. Throw in how his parents were continually uptight and worried sick, adding to his own fear of losing his brother, and he had a clear idea of what Caia had gone through. The difference was that McKenzie was her daughter, so her emotions would've been in line with his parents' feelings. But losing someone you loved hurt like hell no matter what your role in their life was. He knew that from losing Marg. In addition to his guilt and anger, it had hurt beyond description. Had been unbearable, and there was nothing that could've prepared him with waking up every morning knowing she'd gone.

Caia turned in his arm and looked up at him. 'Let's stop being sad and carry on with having a good time.'

Leaning in, he placed a light kiss on her lips. 'I agree.'

She blinked and pulled back as colour crept into her cheeks. 'Want another beer? Or a wine?'

Had he embarrassed her in front of her friends? Tough. She was so tantalising he hadn't been able to help himself. He looked around and saw the other couple out on the deck chatting together. He'd thought other couple. He and Caia weren't a couple. Not yet. Probably never. Though he could admit the idea was becoming more interesting every day. And night. He really liked Caia. She fascinated him.

She nudged him. 'Hello?'

'I'll grab another beer and get a taxi when it's time to go home.' The last thing he was doing was getting behind the wheel of his car after a few beers.

'That's a while away yet.' She grinned. 'Unless you've decided steak and salad isn't your thing.'

'I eat just about anything, especially when someone else prepares it.'

Caia moved to the fridge and got out a container of steak. 'Can you take this out to Brett? And these sausages. The kids prefer them to steak, which is a bonus. More for us.'

'I've got the kids chocolate bars for later. Is that all right?' She might not like McKenzie having sweet treats.

'They'll love you forever.'

Was he the donor that helped save her life? He really, really wanted to know. But at the same time, he understood that if he asked Caia if she was willing to find out, they'd be crossing a line in their relationship they couldn't come back from. It could become quite intense between them and be a reason they continued on together rather than the relationship being about themselves and finding love. That was the last thing he wanted. Having lost the woman he'd given his heart to, he had to be absolutely certain the next time he fell in love, it was for all the right reasons. *If* he ever fell in love again.

'Bring that steak over here.' Brett's voice broke into his displaced mind. 'And the sausages, before we have three hungry girls annoying us.'

'Sure thing.' Lockie placed the containers on the barbecue table. 'Want a hand?'

'Could you grab me another beer?'

Soon they were sitting at the outdoor table with

laden plates of yummy salads and delicious steak, and Lockie felt completely at home. Especially with Caia. Away from work where she was all professional, she was another version of herself. Laughing at the silliest things, and watching McKenzie with so much love it made his heart burn. That's what he wanted. From Caia? He wasn't sure, but as he hadn't felt this way about any woman since Marg, he suspected yes. It was all to do with Caia. Could they take this up a notch tonight once the others left? More of those hot kisses? More than kisses? More heat, more touching. Get to know one another intimately? He breathed deep. Time to slow down and take things one step at a time.

'You got any nieces or nephews?' Izzy asked him.

He shook his head. 'My brother hasn't found the right woman yet. Or so he says. Why do you ask?'

Izzy shrugged. 'Just getting to know you a bit better, I guess.'

Checking him out in case he didn't stack up for Caia? He couldn't feel bad about that. Izzy was being a good friend. 'We're a close-knit family from a long line of doctors. Though no one is ever pressured to take up medicine as a career, it seems to go that way. One of my cousins is a judge, but she's the only one to step outside the medical line in our generation.'

'Interesting,' said Caia. 'Are any of your family nurses? Or been nurses?'

'Both my grandmothers were. Unfortunately not many females studied medicine back in their time. What about your parents?' Stop. Her father did a bunk, remember? 'Sorry. I was wondering about your mother.'

Her smile told him not to worry; he hadn't gone too far. 'She was an office manager for an insurance company most of her working life. Stayed with the same company and never wanted anything more. I think it kept her settled working with the same people most of the time. She didn't like putting herself out there to get knocks on the way through life.'

Izzy looked a little surprised at Caia being so open.

That had to mean Caia felt comfortable with him, didn't it? Who knew? He'd take any good points coming his way, and give some back. 'You didn't inherit those genes.'

Caia's eyes widened. 'I did, but I've learned to fight them wherever possible. Not always easy but the only way I want to be.'

They had that in common. 'I understand completely.' Harry's illness had started the process for him, and Marg had definitely thrown a bomb at him, something which he'd struggled to tough out. Whether he had been as strong as he liked to think, he wasn't sure, but he was getting on with his life, even if not with finding another woman to trust. His gaze cruised to Caia. Yes, she might be the one to help him over the final hurdle. First he had to get to know her a lot better. 'What are you and McKenzie up to tomorrow?'

'Haven't thought that far ahead. I've been promising to take her to the zoo but haven't managed to fit it in yet.'

'Why don't we do that then? I can pick you up, and we can take a picnic with us.' Is that what five-year-olds did? He suddenly realised he had no idea. He knew how kids were meant to be medically at different ages, but not so much about what they got up to. What was the in thing and what was old hat.

'Are you sure?'

'Wouldn't ask if I wasn't.' Why the question?

Caia looked hesitant. 'Okay then.'

'If you don't think it's a good idea, say so.'

After a long moment when he fully expected Caia to say she'd changed her mind about going, she said, 'Thank you. I'm sure we'll have fun.'

That didn't exactly make him feel wonderful, but he'd get over it. Careful Caia to the fore. 'Good.'

'Hey, you two. We're about to head off.'

He hadn't even noticed Izzy and Brett getting their gear together. Showed how much Caia distracted him. He stood up. 'It's been great meeting you both.'

Brett shook his hand. 'We'll do it again soon.' Then he glanced at Caia, who must've nodded, because Brett smiled. 'Our place next time.'

'Hey, great night.' Izzy hugged Caia. 'See you Monday morning.'

Brett rounded up their girls, and they headed out to the car.

Caia sat on the couch with her legs beneath her. McKenzie climbed up beside her, lay her head on Caia's thigh and closed her eyes. 'You fitted in well, Lockie.'

'Hard not to.' It'd been a relaxing evening, no tension whatsoever. 'I like them. They're very easy-going.'

'They always have been like that. They cover each other's deficiencies like they're two halves of the same apple.'

He laughed. 'Apple, eh? Do they know that's what you think?'

'No way. I'd never hear the end of it.' She gently rubbed McKenzie's head. 'Bedtime, my girl.'

'No. I want to stay here with you and Lockie.'

'It's late, and you've had a big day. You're going to bed.'

'I don't want to,' she grizzled.

But when Caia got up and lifted McKenzie to her feet, she toddled along beside her mum with no more complaints.

Lockie headed to the kitchen to rinse the plates

and cutlery before putting them in the dishwasher. He didn't want Caia getting up in the morning to do it or staying up late because of the mess.

'You didn't have to do that.' Caia had returned.

'Maybe not, but I wanted to.' He moved around the bench and reached for her. 'I've had a great time.' He gazed at her, drinking in her lovely face and that riotous hair that made him hot. 'I really have.'

Her mouth widened into one her beautiful smiles.

His toes curled, and his heart expanded. His mouth covered hers for a brief kiss.

Caia kissed him back, her mouth opening for him, her tongue playing tag with his.

Heat rose throughout his body. This was wonderful. He couldn't have been happier. Caia was accepting him. He lifted his head and said, 'You're so beautiful.'

She stared at him as though he'd lost his mind. She pulled back. 'Sure.'

'I mean it, Caia. I wouldn't have said it otherwise.' What was wrong?

She was still staring at him, a big question mark in her eyes. Then she sighed. 'I'm sorry, Lockie. I'm sure you mean it. If only I wasn't so distrustful of men who say things like that.' There was a load of sadness behind her words.

'Tell me more, Caia. I'd really like to know what, who, has caused you to feel like this.' He pulled a stool out from the bench and sat down so he wasn't hovering over her. 'Please.'

Parking that curvy butt on another stool, she stared at the floor for a long moment. Then, raising her head, she locked fierce eyes on him. 'My ex used to tell me I was beautiful, among other lovely things, but he never meant a word of it.'

He wanted to tell her again that he had meant it, but Caia held her hand up in a stop gesture.

'We met when Garth was doing seasonal work on a vineyard here. His visa only had a few months to go, and he wanted residency. I was the idiot who believed it when he said he loved me.'

'McKenzie's father?'

She nodded, those red bangs flicking over her shoulders. 'Strange, but he didn't use her as an excuse to stay. If anything, he used her as an excuse to leave, saying he didn't ever want children. Something I've never understood. I'm in two minds about how I feel. I know what it's like to grow up without a father, but I also doubt Garth would've been a good parent. He's too selfish.'

'Do you think he's still in the country?'

'No idea. I haven't seen him since the day I told him I was pregnant. For all I know, he's conned another woman into believing she's everything to him.' Her bitterness was raw and hung between them like a huge warning sign. *Don't mess with me.*

No, but he would show her she hadn't scared

him off wanting to get closer. Standing up, he crossed to hug her, holding her tight. 'You're amazing. To think what you've been through as a mum, and you still smile.'

She slumped against him. 'Thank you.'

He smiled into her hair. He'd got it right.

Caia stayed tucked in against Lockie for a few moments, but finally drew away. Otherwise she'd never move except to drag him down to her bedroom and have her way with that wickedly sexy body. But she mustn't. Not yet. Hearing him say she was beautiful had woken her up to the fact that despite wanting him, she wasn't ready to take a chance on him letting her down. And she knew she was already feeling something stronger than physical attraction for him.

There was so much to like about him. To love about him? Yes, probably, and that was the scary part. She wasn't ready to let go the grip she had on her trust. She wanted to, but it wasn't happening overnight. She'd had a great evening with Lockie and her friends, ignoring the tightness that held her heart long enough to make the most of it. But when those words came out of his mouth, she retreated right back to her normal approach to relationships. She was not going to be conned into believing she was loveable. Whoever she fell for would have to prove she was special to him. He could not have a hidden agenda of saying things that were meant to tempt her to let go of all her restraints.

Did this mean she should cancel tomorrow's trip to the zoo? But why should she? She wanted to believe Lockie when he said he meant it, and a part of her did. He often said it as he saw it, at work and with the girls earlier when he'd held his ground, not just saying what he knew they wanted to hear. She didn't want to walk away from a chance at happiness, but she wasn't keen to rush it and fall flat on her face again. She did not want McKenzie getting the wrong idea about why Lockie was going with them. 'About tomorrow.'

Lockie took her hands in his. Before she could say anything more, he interjected with, 'We're going to take McKenzie to the zoo and give her a great time. And enjoy ourselves along the way. All right?'

Surprisingly, it *did* feel right. 'Absolutely.' Maybe she didn't realise how much she wanted to move on from the past and have those wonderful opportunities she used to dream about. Whatever the answer, she was going to take a chance on Lockie. Only way to go.

'I'll pick you up about eleven thirty if that suits? I've got to go into the practise first to do some jobs.'

'Perfect.' She knew he was always busy keeping on top of rosters, paperwork and all the other requirements of a busy business. She'd picked up from Dave that Lockie tended to take over so he and Katie could have time with their families on the weekends.

'I'll be going, let you get some beauty sleep—not that you need any.'

Damn, but she wanted him to stay. To continue that kiss and add to the experience by following on with some mind-blowing sex. But her *be careful* hat was firmly in place, and as that had kept her on the straight and narrow, she'd go with the flow this time. Stretching up, she kissed Lockie lightly. 'Thank you for being so understanding.'

Her knees weakened as he smiled and said, 'No problem,' before walking out the door.

Another tick for Lockie. He was gaining plenty of those all too easily. More than that, she was happy he was.

'Mummy.'

McKenzie. Caia's heart slipped. It was all very well getting excited about Lockie, but what about her girl? McKenzie was inclined to overreact to people and include them too quickly in whatever she was thinking. Time for a wee talk. 'Coming, sweetheart.'

McKenzie's eyes lit up when she walked into her bedroom. 'I liked the barbecue, Mummy. Can we have another one?'

'Of course we will.' It wasn't a rare occurrence. Sitting on the edge of the bed, she thought about how to say this without making out Lockie was important. 'Would you like to go to the zoo tomorrow?'

'Yeees.' McKenzie bounced up and down under her bedcovers. 'Can Jessie and Jodie come?'

'Not this time. We're going with Lockie.'

Her wee face dipped. A sign that she didn't see him as anyone special? 'Why?'

'The girls are busy with their mum and dad. You know I work for Lockie?'

'You told me.'

She nodded. 'I did. Well, we are also friends, but that doesn't mean I'll see a lot of him. Tomorrow he's not working, so he's coming with us to the zoo, but he won't do things like that very often.'

'That's okay. What animals are we going to see?'

Caia sighed with relief. So far McKenzie was excited about the zoo, which was not a surprise. Long may that last. 'Giraffes, lions, bears, monkeys. Lots of different animals.'

'You have to take pictures for me, Mummy.'

Leaning in, she kissed her girl. 'Lots and lots, I promise. Now you need to go to sleep so that tomorrow gets here faster.' She doubted she'd get much sleep herself. She'd done her best to explain things to McKenzie without getting in deep. If McKenzie appeared to be thinking Lockie was more important than she should, all Caia could do now was to continue to reiterate what she'd just said and hope it was enough.

CHAPTER SEVEN

On the way home from the zoo, Lockie felt more relaxed than he'd been in a long time. All because of a day out with Caia and her daughter, having a picnic and wandering around looking at the animals that enthralled McKenzie. Who'd have thought something so ordinary could make him feel this way? Certainly not him.

McKenzie must've felt much the same, because she was sound asleep in her car seat. As for Caia? He glanced sideways and laughed. She was yawning.

'What's funny?' she asked.

'Seems I'm boring company. Neither of you can stay awake.'

'That's fine. It's you who has to be focused behind the steering wheel,' she retorted with a smile that went straight to his gut. Like most of her smiles did.

'We spent a lot longer at the zoo than I thought we would. McKenzie was smitten with every animal she saw. Didn't matter whether if it was a bear or giraffe.'

'She'd love to have a puppy, but we haven't got the space or the time required for walks.'

'Bet that doesn't make you popular.'

'I was hoping it might be a passing fad, but not so. I'd like a dog, but now's not the time. Have you ever had one?'

A picture of Jack filled his mind. 'An English springer spaniel. Got him as a pup, and could he do zoomies. They're known for them, but at the time, I had no idea what it meant. I just thought we'd gotten a mad-energetic dog.' His parents brought home Jack when Harry was ill as something for Lockie to focus on other than his brother being sick. When Harry was back on his feet, they both spent equal amounts of time with the pup as he grew into a very affectionate dog. 'He drove us crazy, but we adored him all the same.'

Caia stretched her legs as far as possible and lifted her arms over her head with another yawn. 'I'm tired, yet we haven't done that much.'

'You had a busy week at work, and from what I've seen, you don't exactly sit down to relax very often.' She was always on the go, especially at work, even when she didn't have patients to see. 'We don't expect you to be busy for the sake of it.'

'It's how I am.'

Along with beautiful and sexy. He'd keep that

to himself, especially after her reaction the last time he'd told her.

Not so easy to stick to that a couple of hours later when McKenzie was tucked up in bed, out to the world, and Caia sat beside him on the couch with her feet curled underneath her and a glass of the pinot noir he'd bought in hand. She looked utterly wonderful.

'Thanks for a great day,' he said.

A frown appeared between those bewitching eyes. 'I should be thanking you. McKenzie doesn't get to do exciting things like that very often. As for me, I really enjoyed spending time with you. We seem to gel almost too easily.'

'Why *too* easily? Is that a problem?' He wanted to know how she felt about them spending time together. Maybe it was the occasion to find out whether they were headed in the same direction or if he should bow out while he still could without getting hurt, or at least control the degree of hurt.

Caia sat up straighter. 'Not at all.' She spoke sharply. 'I like how we get along so well. It's not something I'm used to, that's all.' She winced. 'What I mean is, I usually resist getting too close to people, and with you, that hasn't been the case so far.'

He'd certainly got an answer to his questions. 'I'm glad you feel that way, because I've also felt immediately comfortable spending this time with you, which I'll also admit I'm not used to. Something we have in common.' A change of subject was required before she asked what he meant. He was not ready to talk about Marg. The last thing he needed was Caia feeling sorry for him, or worse, having her asking if he'd noticed Marg was acting strangely or differently. That'd bring up the guilt again, and he was determined to leave it behind him. Of course, if he and Caia did become an item, then they would need to have that conversation, but not yet.

Nothing came to mind to talk about. Instead he sipped his wine and studied Caia. He didn't get far. That amazing splash of red hair stalled his heart and sent heat racing around his body. 'Caia.'

Her eyes widened. 'Yes, Lockie?'

'I'm going to kiss you. Is that okay?'

She put her glass aside and turned to face him full on. 'Definitely.'

Then his lips were covering hers, and they were kissing like there was no tomorrow. As though they'd both dropped all restraint and had to make the most of this time together. He held her head gently and kissed her hard, receiving her deep kiss with vigour. She tasted of pinot noir and sex. He wanted more. Lots more.

His hands moved of their own accord, down to her waist, then to her breasts, cupping their warm softness. His fingers tweaked her nipples, which hardened instantly. 'Oh, Caia.'

'Lockie,' she whispered against his mouth. 'I need you. With me. In me.'

His answer was to place her hand on his need tenting the front of his jeans.

Her hand was pushing against his erection, her fingers rubbing him through the denim. At this rate, he was going to come too soon. 'Caia, slow down. I want to touch you, feel your skin under my hands, hold your breasts.' He couldn't go on, his need using up his breath.

She flipped onto her back, her feet pushing him out of the way so she could stretch out. 'Come on then.'

He stopped. 'What about McKenzie?' The last thing he wanted was her appearing in the doorway demanding to know what they were doing.

'I can't believe I didn't think about her.' Guilt flickered across Caia's face and was soon gone as she reached a hand out to him. 'Help me up. She won't wake up, but just in case, we're going to my room. There's a lock on the door.'

'You sure?' If she said no, he'd be gutted, but he also knew she wanted him as much as he wanted her. That would go a long way in appeasing him if she changed her mind.

She kissed him. Not lightly but hard and demanding. 'Come on.'

Caia jerked the covers off her bed before pulling Lockie down with her to carry on learning all she could about that amazing body she'd been wondering about for weeks. This beat going to the zoo anytime. Though that was what had led to Lockie being here with her, so maybe they could go again. Sooner rather than later.

The sound of McKenzie's favourite song broke through the steamy air.

Lockie jerked upwards. 'What's that?'

Her heart sank. 'My phone.'

'Ignore it.'

Oh, how she wanted to. 'Would you if you were on call?' She leaned over to grab the bloody interfering instrument. 'I have a patient due any day.'

Lockie sat up and scrubbed at his face as if he could remove the need that was so obvious. 'Tell me it's the zoo saying we dropped our lunch wrapper on the grass.'

If she hadn't been so wound up with desire for him, she'd have laughed, but it wasn't happening. She didn't recognise the number on her screen, another pointer to it being a patient. 'Hello, Caia Johnstone speaking.'

'Caia, it's Melanie Smeith. I'm in labour, six minutes between contractions.'

They hadn't met yet as Melanie cancelled her appointment on Thursday due to her mother having a fall and needing to go to hospital. Closing her eyes, Caia breathed deep and said, 'Right, where are you?' So much for getting down and dirty with Lockie. That had taken a flying leap out the window.

'At home, but Alex is getting the car out of the garage to take me to the facility as we speak.'

'I'll meet you there. Don't rush. Contractions six minutes apart means you've got a little way to go.' She looked at Lockie and saw the disappointment filling his face. *Sorry*, she mouthed. She'd pulled away from going too far last time they shared that amazing kiss. This time a patient was doing the honours. She should have been grateful but couldn't quite manage that.

He laid a hand on her thigh and squeezed gently. 'Can't be helped,' he whispered.

'Thanks, Caia,' said Melanie. 'Sorry I haven't met you yet, but seems we're about to make up for that in the coming hours.'

Hours. Yes. She could sneak thirty minutes in bed with Lockie, and everyone would be happy. Except she wouldn't be, because she loved the after sex time when she snuggled into the man she was with, feeling wonderful. She also had to sort out McKenzie before she went anywhere. 'It's all right, Melanie. See you shortly.' She hung up and shook her head. 'Who'd have thought it?'

'The joys of our careers.' Lockie smiled woefully. He stood up and reached for his discarded shirt. 'Do you want me to stay here with McKenzie? It wouldn't be a problem.'

No way. That meant McKenzie getting closer

to Lockie when *she* still didn't know where they were going with this, other than having sex. Which they still hadn't, she reminded herself unhappily. 'Thanks, but I've got it covered. My neighbour will come over and stay the night, and I'll top up her money jar. She's at university, and every dollar counts.'

'Who's your patient? Is she one of ours?' Lockie asked as he pulled on his shirt.

'Yes, she is. Melanie Smeith. This is her second baby.'

'Third. She lost her first one at childbirth six years ago when she was living in Australia.'

'That wasn't in the records. What was the cause, do you know?'

'The umbilical cord was partially pulled away from the baby's stomach. I don't know all the details, but it took Melanie a while to find the courage to try again.'

'I bet it did. She didn't sound too fazed talking to me, but she might be good at hiding her feelings.' She tugged a brush through the mess that was her hair and banged the brush back down. 'Oh, Lockie. Why tonight?'

He pulled her into a hug. 'Know what you mean, but there's not a lot we can do about it.' He tapped her bottom lightly. 'You'd better get a wiggle on.'

Smiling sadly, she flicked through her contact

list and pressed the number for her neighbour. 'Paula, are you at home?'

'Hi, Caia. Guess this means you're heading out to bring another wee one into the world.' Paula chuckled. 'I'll be there in five.' Click. Gone.

'What do you do if she can't come over?' Lockie asked.

'Depends whether it's day or night. Daytime, I check to see if Izzy can have McKenzie, and at night, I take her with me. I'm sure you know there's a room put aside at the facility for midwives' kids in those circumstances. If I'm dealing with a complicated birth, one of the nurses or aides usually keeps an eye on her for me.'

'If you ever get stuck, call me.' Lockie was genuine and won another tick from her.

Somehow she knew he'd never deliberately let her down if they became a couple. But then, she'd thought Garth wouldn't either—until he did, thereby proving she hadn't known him at all. Would she ever be able to trust a man again without thinking he had ulterior motives? She had to or she was going to miss out on some of the best things in life—like constant love, having her other half there for her, and her for him. She didn't have time to carry on with the list. She had a baby to deliver. 'I'll call Annie tomorrow so she can get in touch with my patients if I'm still tied up.'

Lockie nodded. 'She'll rebook the women for

the afternoon if necessary, or the following day.' He sighed. 'I'll get out of your hair so you can get ready to go where you're needed. See you sometime tomorrow.' His brief kiss felt full of disappointment.

Her body was aching with the same emotion. 'Sorry, Lockie.'

He tapped her nose. 'No problem.' Then he was gone, taking a piece of her heart with him.

Paula rushed through the door. 'Hey, well-timed. I only got home ten minutes before you phoned.'

Something was working out, then. 'Thanks, Paula. As usual, I have no idea how long I'll be.'

'If you're not home when I have to leave for university, I'll drop McKenzie off at Izzy's.'

She was so lucky with Paula. As she was with Izzy and Brett. She'd be lost without them. Working kept her sane—most of the time. And gave her a sense of being worthwhile while paying the bills. 'You're a champ.' Snatching up her bag, and keys she headed away, her mind flipping to her patient and what lay ahead.

'Melanie, try not to push. Your cervix isn't open far enough yet. At least one more centimetre to go,' Caia warned.

'It's taking forever.' It was a familiar rant with patients at this stage of birthing.

She'd felt the same when McKenzie was born,

despite a short labour compared to many. 'You're doing great. I don't think you've got too long to go now.' Thankfully it was a straightforward birth, like Melanie's previous one. But because of the trouble with her first baby, Caia was keeping a sharp eye on everything. 'Hopefully baby will crown soon.'

Alex held his wife's hand. 'You're wonderful, sweetheart.'

'You can have the next one so you know how wonderful,' Melanie snapped, then grimaced as a contraction ripped through her.

'Hell no. Blokes can't cope with childbirth.'

Caia couldn't help laughing, risking a growl from her patient. 'Glad you recognise the fact.' For someone she'd met an hour ago, he was easygoing, even when his wife was in agony and blaming him for everything.

'Staying safe,' he muttered and wrapped his arms around Melanie to help her stand up.

'Rub my back. It's hurting big-time.' Melanie fell against him. 'I'm not doing this again.'

'You said that last time.'

'I mean it this time.'

Alex rolled his eyes. 'Sure.' His hands were massaging Melanie's lower back with a purpose suggesting he'd done it often.

'You have back problems?' Caia asked her.

'The result of being thrown off a horse when

I was eight. Ended up in hospital for a month. Ahhh. Sod this, Alex.'

After waiting out the contraction, Caia checked Melanie's pulse and then her BP before another contraction made itself felt. 'All good. No hurry, but when you're back on the bed, I'll check your cervix to see if it's widened further.' After crossing to the bench, she updated the notes on the laptop. Everything was going well. Her first birthing here and she couldn't be more comfortable. Being a midwife and watching babies come into the world was amazing. Her dream job. She sighed. As long as she wasn't tempting trouble with those thoughts.

'Ahhhh.' Melanie clutched her belly. 'Ahhhh. That's stronger than the others.'

'Lie down.' Pulling on gloves, Caia got down on her knees at the end of the bed while Melanie lay back and spread her legs wide. 'Progress. Baby's crowning. The contractions should start coming faster any minute.'

'Bang-on,' Melanie groaned as a contraction seized her.

Everything sped up from then on, and forty minutes later, Caia was easing baby Faye out from her mother's cervix and cutting the umbilical cord. 'Well done, Melanie.'

After wiping Faye's face clear of mucus, she placed the baby into her mother's arms. 'There you go, Mum and Dad.' She stood back, trying to deny the moisture in her eyes as she saw the joy and love in Melanie's and Alex's faces. It was a wondrous moment she never got enough of. Would she be lucky enough to experience it for herself again? If Lockie became part of her life, would he want children? She presumed so but didn't really know. It wasn't the first question she asked a man when she began dating him. Lockie's gentle approach to McKenzie suggested he liked children and therefore wouldn't be averse to having his own, but as she kept reminding herself, she was useless at reading the men she became interested in.

Clearing her throat, she said, 'I need to remove the umbilical cord, Melanie. Another push or two required.' Back on her knees, Caia dealt with the cord and wiped Melanie clean.

'I'll weigh Faye before I go out in the staff room and leave you both to get to know your girl. Come and get me if you need anything, including coffee or tea, Alex.' Giving parents space to be with their baby was important, because that time was special. It also gave her a chance to overcome the emotions rolling through her and get back on track.

Walking out of the room, she checked her phone and saw it was five thirty. The night had gone by fast. The message icon indicated she'd received a text twenty minutes ago. After she tapped the screen, Lockie's name appeared.

His message read, How's it going? Any sign of junior?

She started replying, then paused. To hell with it. He was obviously awake. She pushed the phone icon and waited for his husky voice to tickle her insides.

'Hey, you doing all right?' Lockie asked.

That voice made her sigh happily. 'Everything went well. Baby arrived fifteen minutes ago, healthy and weighing in at four point four kilos.'

'Awesome. Congratulations on your first birth with our clinic.' Lockie sounded almost excited. Was that because their new venture was now off the ground and running as they'd hoped?

'Cheers, Lockie. It has been an exciting few hours, but most births are. I'm going to drink tea and get my breath back. Figuratively speaking, that is. I always become emotional after a birth.' *Stop. You're telling him too much about yourself.* But how were they to progress if she didn't open up a little?

'I understand what you're saying. I only witnessed a few births while training, but they got to me every time.'

'Why are you up so early?' Or was this his regular wakeup hour?

'I didn't get a lot of sleep and in the end gave up and decided to do some work on a plan I'm drafting for the GP association.'

At the mention of lack of sleep, a yawn gripped

her. Now she'd finished helping bring Faye into the world, she was tired. Another common occurrence when she put everything she could into making sure everything went well. But she had a full day ahead with patients to see and two home calls to make. 'I'm going to take a shower and change into something less wrinkled and grubby before I do anything else.'

'Are you popping home before the staff meeting?'

Damn, she'd forgotten about that. 'Probably not. Paula will drop McKenzie at Izzy's on her way into the city, and she'll be gone before I can get home as I can't leave Melanie yet. She's going to stay here for the day, so I can check her out before I go home tonight.' The day nurse would keep an eye on her and baby and let Caia know if anything was off-centre throughout the day.

'Then I'll pick up something from the bakery for breakfast and see you when you get to the clinic.'

'You don't have to do that.'

'Why do you always react negatively when I offer to do something for you?'

She chewed her bottom lip, not wanting to answer.

'You're not alone, Caia. It's what anyone at the practise would do, and me in particular,' he added with a lightness in his voice that hadn't been there a moment ago.

She wasn't used to letting a man run around after her, because she'd decided long ago they only did it when they wanted more from her than she was prepared to give. But again, Lockie sounded genuine, and she had to accept it or stop seeing him outside work, and she couldn't find it within her to do that. 'Breakfast would be lovely. I'm starving. And thank you. I'm sorry for my reaction.' It had been automatic, something else she had to stop doing if she wanted that happy-ever-after life she dreamed of.

'No problem. See you later.'

'Bye,' she replied, feeling confused. Happy and worried. *Drop the worry and focus on the happy.*

'That Garth has a lot to answer for,' Lockie mused to himself as he sat down in front of the computer in his examining room and clicked on patients for the day. Caia's wariness around Lockie suggested she might never tell him more about herself. As the screen filled with his list, he could imagine her tense face and felt a strong need to protect her come over him. She was a kind, generous woman who gave her all for her daughter, her friends and her patients. How could that bastard hurt her when she gave so much of herself?

But he knew too well how possible it was. Not everyone out there thought about the needs of their partner or their friends. Caia didn't readily give herself away. She'd withdrawn the night they shared their first kiss. As for last night, she was more than ready to go the distance and have sex with him. She hadn't looked relieved when the phone call interrupted them, appearing as devastated as he'd been. But this morning, she'd held back over something as simple as him buying breakfast to have at work.

'You're a mystery, Caia Johnstone. One I'm enjoying unravelling even if it's going to be a slow process.'

He had no doubt she'd be hot in bed, and there'd be no holding back then. The way she'd pressed against him, felt for his need and rubbed him said she wouldn't put on the brakes once they started. Except for that damned phone call. He'd wanted to snatch the phone out of her hand and throw it on the floor, which said where he'd been. He knew too well that she couldn't walk away from a patient, even if she'd been able to call someone else to take over.

'Morning, Lockie.' Katie appeared in the doorframe. 'You're early. Another sleepless night?' she smirked.

He'd only started lying awake for hours on end since Caia came into his life. For some stupid reason, he'd mentioned not sleeping well during a meeting with her and Dave. They weren't letting him hear the end of their ribbing. Of course they were guessing why he wasn't sleeping well, and the point was, they were right. 'Caia had her first delivery at the clinic last night. Melanie Smeith had a baby girl early this morning. All went well.'

'That's wonderful. I'm glad she didn't have any difficulties like she did with the first one.'

'If you're talking about Melanie, it was a straightforward birth,' Caia said from behind Katie. 'Everything went swimmingly, and she and Alex are stoked.'

Katie stepped back to make room for her. 'You hadn't met them before last night, had you?'

'No, but they were so easy to talk to and made me feel completely relaxed. It's supposed to be the other way round.'

'I'm sure you did the same for them,' Lockie couldn't help saying, and got a wink from Katie. *Thanks, pal.* He did need to get himself under control. Turning back to the screen, he said, 'There're croissants for everyone in the break room.' See, he was looking out for everyone, not only Caia. *Tell that to someone who believes you.*

'Yummy,' Caia said. 'I'm absolutely starving. It wasn't a physically hard night, but it was a long one, and I need food. Now.'

'I brought jam and honey as well.'

'Are you joining us?' she asked.

No. He had to get his head on straight before his first patient—who was at least half an hour away. 'I'll be there shortly.' His pen flicked across the desk as irritation took over. He couldn't think clearly whenever Caia was around. This was the craziest, most mixed-up state he'd been in for years. How could one woman do this when he was usually in control of his emotions? Or had been, except when coming to grips with losing Marg. He'd loved Marg like there was no one else on the planet, yet here he was wondering if he might find something similar with Caia. There was a long way to go before he knew the answer to that, and first he had to decide if it was what he wanted. If it wasn't, he had to back away now. Not next week, not after hot sex, not later when they'd been on more dates. He had to do it today. Now. No mucking around trying to keep two balls in the air while he made up his mind. Since the thought of getting hurt again kept nudging him, he knew which way he had to go.

His heart crunched. It wasn't easy, but he had to look out for himself. By doing that, he'd also be making sure neither Caia nor McKenzie was hurt. Or was that his excuse for not taking a chance with Caia? If he was going to fall in love again, he had an inkling she could be the woman he'd cherish more than anyone.

A plate with a croissant appeared before him. Caia said, 'Thought I'd bring you one as they're disappearing fast.'

'Thanks.'

'No, thank you.' She waited for a moment but

he couldn't think of anything to say that didn't show he was in a turmoil, so he kept quiet.

She said, 'I'll carry on. First patient's due in ten.'

'Mine too,' he told her.

CHAPTER EIGHT

'CAIA, GOT A MINUTE? I've got a patient I'd like you to talk to.' Lockie sat on the corner of her desk.

'That's what I'm here for.' They'd hardly talked over the last three days, passing each other in the practise or downing coffee in the break room between patients, but nothing personal. It wasn't chilly between them, more like two busy people passing on the street. But strange all the same.

'Karen Kellerman is seventeen and nearly six months pregnant. She hasn't seen a midwife or GP about the pregnancy until now. She's having some spotting but only wants a woman to examine her.'

'That's where I come in.'

'Yes. I explained your role as a midwife, and she says she'll enrol with you. I've pointed out that first the cause of the spotting has to be found.'

'Is anyone with her?'

'No. Unfortunately her mother couldn't get away from work.'

Caia's stomach tightened for the girl she hadn't even met yet. 'What a shame. It's hard being pregnant, and having to go through an exam alone is sad.'

Lockie fixed his gaze on her, a question in his eyes.

'Yes, I did it alone. My mother wasn't often there for me.' That's all she was saying. 'I'm presuming there isn't a partner.'

'You're right. Karen went to a party with friends, and this is the result.'

'Is she going to keep the baby?'

'No idea. I'm arranging for her to see someone from community services. It's hard to think what lies ahead for Karen. She says she's always been focused on studying because she wants to get ahead with a career.'

'Then here's hoping she has a lot of help and gets back on track after baby's born. Where is she?'

'Waiting to meet you in my room.'

Standing up, Caia sighed. 'Let's do this.'

'You'll be good for Karen. She likes straight talking despite coming across as shy.'

Damn, but she could do with Lockie by her side all the time. He knew how to make her feel good about herself. 'I learnt the hard way to be open and honest.' All right, not always open, but definitely honest.

'Life's lessons, eh?'

Opening the door into his room, he let her to go in first. 'Hello, Karen. I'm Caia, the midwife Dr Lockie told you about.'

Sitting hunched up as though she was trying to hide her baby bump, the girl had dark shadows under her eyes, and her mouth was so sad. 'Thank you for seeing me.'

'No problem. Would you like to come along to my room so we can talk about what lies ahead for you during your pregnancy?'

Karen nodded and stood up. 'I haven't seen a midwife.'

'I'll give you a thorough examination and talk you through everything I do.' It wasn't easy for young girls to undergo an internal exam, but there was no alternative.

'Okay.'

Glancing at Lockie, Caia received a smile.

Thanks, he mouthed.

It was what she was here for, but it still felt good having him say that. She was getting needy if she required Lockie's approval for everything she did around here. She gave him the thumbs-up and joined Karen in the corridor. 'Along here. Lockie said you're studying hard at college. What do you want to do when you leave there?'

'I want to be a nurse, but guess I can't now.'

'You can be whatever you want. It might take longer than you planned and a lot of hard work, but believe me, you can do it.'

'You think?'

'I know. I've seen other patients think they've lost an opportunity to make a great life for themselves and their baby, and then watched them turn their thinking around and obtain that dream.'

Karen blinked. 'Thanks. I'd better wait till I get through this first.'

'Take a seat.' Caia closed the door behind them and sat down to create a file for Karen. 'Since you're a patient at the practise, I only need your full name to get started. Then I'll check your blood pressure. Have you had one done before?'

'No.'

'It's painless. I put a cuff around your arm and pump it tight, which can be uncomfortable, but it doesn't take long to get a result. Slip the sleeve of your right arm up as high as possible.'

Karen seemed fascinated with the procedure, keeping her eye on every move Caia made, no longer focused on hiding her tummy.

'Normal, as expected.' Caia ripped the cuff off and noted down the result. 'Sometimes the BP can be slightly high during pregnancy, especially in the last trimester. Nothing to worry about at the moment, though. I understand you're about six months pregnant.'

'Yes. It happened late March.' She faltered to a stop, drew a breath and continued. 'It's the only time I've done that with a guy.'

'It happens more often than you'd think these days despite all the contraceptive drugs available.'

'I never got them because I didn't think I'd have sex with someone since I wasn't dating.' When she opened up, Karen seemed to say anything that came into her head. Better than holding back. Especially if she hadn't had anyone to talk to.

'I need you to lie on the bed so I can feel around your tummy. Then I'll do an internal examination. Do you know what I mean by that?'

'You're going to look inside me.'

After the examination was finished, they both sat back at the desk. 'What now?' Karen asked, drawing circles on her thigh with a forefinger.

'As far as the pregnancy goes, nothing. Everything's normal. I suggest you visit me every month so I can keep tabs on things and reassure you if you have any concerns.'

'Yes, please.' Karen stared at the floor. 'I want to be a nurse so badly.' Tears poured down her cheeks. 'I've been stupid. How could I have got pregnant so easily?'

Caia reached over to touch her hand. 'Don't be hard on yourself, Karen. We all make mistakes, some worse than others, but you'll cope. I know you will.'

'How?'

'First things first. Meet the woman Dr Lockie's arranging to help you and discuss all your concerns with her. She'll have suggestions for you to think about. You can call me anytime too.'

Karen stood up. 'Thanks. I'd better get going.'

'Where to?'

'School, I suppose.' Her enthusiasm was worse than a wet blanket.

'Why don't you hang around until I've finished with my patients this morning? Then I'll take you down to the maternity hospital and show you round. That's where you'll have your baby,' Caia added.

For the first time, Karen's eyes lit up. 'You'd do that?'

'More than that.' She dug into her bag and pulled out some cash. 'There's a cafe over the road. Get yourself a coffee or whatever you prefer while you wait for me.' Then she added to the cash. 'Get me a cappuccino while you're at it.' Anything to keep that smile on the girl's face.

'Karen looked a lot happier when she left than she had first thing this morning,' Lockie commented later in the break room as everyone downed lunch.

Caia smiled happily. 'I took her with me to the midwifery facility. Figured it might help her to see how everything works. I got the feeling she was more interested in it all from a nursing perspective. She intends on studying nursing when she finishes school, but right now that's up in the air.'

'Early days. I think she's going to turn out to be one strong young lady.'

'Are you talking about Karen Kellerman?' Val asked. 'I saw her in here earlier. She seemed to be hiding within herself.'

'That's her. She's pregnant and feeling very alone. Lockie's organised community care for her, and she's very grateful.' Caia looked directly at him and nodded. 'She says you're very kind.'

He should have laughed, but he couldn't. It felt good to know he'd helped someone in their black moment. 'Thanks.' Hopefully one day Caia would move on from the cause of those dark moments that sometimes appeared in her face, and be able to put the past behind her. If he'd helped, then that was good, but it didn't mean he was moving in on her. 'She's young to be facing pregnancy. I know her mother's there, but she's a very busy lawyer with little time to spare,' he said.

She winced, and a shadow crept into her gaze. 'I wondered what the problem might be.'

Judging from the little she'd told him, that was something she understood. And she was running solo with McKenzie. Lucky she had Izzy and Brett onside or he couldn't imagine how she'd manage, though he knew without a doubt she would. He wanted to be there for her too.

Caia stood up. 'Time I got back to work. I've

got two house calls to make this afternoon, and then I'm done.'

'You might get a full night's sleep tonight.' Unless he knocked on her door to continue what Melanie had interrupted last Sunday. As if he'd do that. As much as he'd like to, he needed some sleep too or he was going to fall asleep at his desk any day soon.

'Hopefully,' Caia answered as she walked away, leaving him in no doubt he wasn't about to be invited around to finish what they'd started.

After getting another coffee, he sat back down to discuss rosters with the nurses at the table.

Annie flew into the room. 'Lockie, Caia needs you fast. Judith Mayes has fallen to the floor in the waiting room and isn't responding.'

Up on his feet in a shot, he raced out to the waiting room to find Judith sprawled over the carpet with Caia on her knees beside her, checking her neck pulse while lifting one of her eyelids.

Another patient knelt opposite Caia, holding Judith's hand. 'Doc, it doesn't look good.'

'Move aside, Dan.' He dropped down beside the man and glanced at Caia. 'What do you think?'

'I'm not a nurse, but wonder if she's had a stroke. The left side of her face seems to have dropped.'

'She was complaining of a bad headache,' Dan told them.

That certainly pointed to a stroke. *Well done, Caia*, Lockie thought as he asked Judith, 'Can you hear me?'

'Yys.'

Slurred speech was another indicator. He reached for her left hand. 'Can you feel me touching your hand?'

'Nnoo.'

'Want me to call an ambulance?' Caia asked.

'Please. Tell them we think Judith's had a stroke.' He looked around for one of the nurses who'd followed him out of the tearoom. 'Val, can you get a vial of tPA?' Tissue plasminogen activator would help break up any clots that were causing the stroke. 'Grab the defib too. Just in case.' He didn't have to say in case of what. Everyone was aware Judith could have heart failure.

'On it.'

'Keep checking the pulse, Caia.' The last thing they wanted was a clot to cause Judith's to heart to stop.

Caia was talking to the ambulance call centre but nodded at him and placed a finger on Judith's neck. She mightn't be a nurse, but she was still calm in tricky situations, something he admired.

Val was back with the tPA and quickly administered it.

'Dan, can you ask someone at the main desk to get a pillow and blanket?' Lockie asked to give the man something to do.

'Sure.'

'Ambulance on the way,' Caia said as she took the pulse under her finger. Then, 'One hundred thirty.'

'Tachycardia.'

'What else can we do?' Caia asked.

'Roll her into a recovery position and keep her warm until the paramedics get here.' *And cross our fingers nothing else goes wrong.* He hated these moments when he could do little more than wait.

A soft touch on his wrist made him look up into Caia's eyes.

'Hey.' She nodded, understanding what he felt.

'I'll get a list of Judith's medications for the paramedic to take with her. Val, take my place. Call me if anything changes.'

Caia was taking the pulse again. 'No change,' she noted.

'Good.'

Half an hour later, Judith was transferred to an ambulance while Lockie filled the paramedics in on what had happened before handing over the notes he'd printed about her medications and previous health issues. As the ambulance drove away, he watched Caia come out and head for her car on her way to her first house call. She gave him a wave as she left.

The throbbing in his heart increased. Maybe he would call in on Caia after he finished up for the day after all. There was no getting away from the fact he had to see more of her and wanted to spend as much time as possible in her company.

'Good night, sweetheart. Sleep tight, and don't let the bedbugs bite.' Caia kissed McKenzie on her forehead.

'Have we got bugs in our beds, Mummy? Everyone says they're horrid.'

'No, we haven't got bedbugs, my girl. Our beds are very clean. It's an old saying, that's all.' Had one of McKenzie's friends dealt with them? More likely it was just the kids having fun.

'I'm glad. I don't want to get bites all over me like Mark did. He said he'd been bitten by fleas from his dog.'

So that's where the story came from. Kids, eh? 'Okay, lights out time.' Enough of McKenzie's delaying tactics.

'Can't I read?'

'You've already been reading. It's getting late, and you've got a big day tomorrow.' Friday sports was McKenzie's favourite day.

McKenzie grinned. 'Yay, running races and jumping over hurdles like horses.'

'A little less of the horse thing and more running, please.' The thought of her girl getting caught up in a hurdle, no matter how low it was, didn't make her feel great. A broken leg was not on the agenda. It wouldn't be fair after all McKenzie had had to deal with so far in her life.

'Aww, Mummy, I like jumping.'

'I know.' The last time was when she leapt off the porch and landed face first in the garden. Fortunately no damage was done except to McKenzie's pride, but still. 'Good night,' she said again and switched off the light. 'See you in the morning.'

'Night, Mummy.'

In the kitchen, Caia put the kettle on to make tea and put the dinner plates in the dishwasher. Mundane was good. It gave her time to wind down from the hectic day. First meeting Karen and trying to make life a little easier for her, and then that woman having a stroke in the waiting room. Add in the scheduled patients and she'd had a busier than usual day. Not that she minded. Quite enjoyed it really, except for the fact that others had been suffering. She'd worked with Lockie with both those patients too. He was so easy to work alongside. The nurses made similar comments during her first week, saying she'd have no problems with any of the doctors, and especially Lockie. So it wasn't only her he treated well, but he still made her feel good.

The doorbell chimed.

'Who's that?' She didn't get nighttime callers unless they'd phoned to say they were coming.

As she peeked through the security hole in

the door, a thrill of excitement caught her. Wow. Pulling the door wide, she inhaled hard. 'Hello, Lockie.' What brought him here?

'Hope you don't mind, but I was on my way home when I thought I'd call in to see how you are after the day of surprises.'

'I'm fine. It's been interesting and kept my mind busy.' He looked so gorgeous in his rumpled clothes. His hair appeared as though he'd been running his fingers through it often.

'Can I come in? Or would you prefer I disappeared?' He was grinning, but she sensed he also wasn't sure of her reaction to him turning up unannounced.

She had been so preoccupied with his looks that she'd forgotten they were standing at the front door going nowhere. 'Come in.'

'Phew.' He laughed.

How she loved that deep husky laugh. Sexy as. 'I was making a cuppa. Do you want one, or would you prefer something else?'

'Tea would be great.'

'Plonk your butt on a stool while I finish tidying up.' She could also have given herself a command: *Try to ignore all the longing for his body waking up fast*. Too fast, but it was as though her need had been waiting for him to come back and finish what they'd barely started. If only she hadn't got that call from Melanie the other night. Then she'd know exactly what it was like to get down and dirty with Lockie. Know what making love with him was truly like. Because she believed it would be out of this world for her and wanted it confirmed. Naturally if it was as good as she hoped, then she'd be wanting more—and more.

'The kettle's been boiling for a while there,' Lockie said with a laugh.

She shook her head to get rid of the imaginings going on inside. Time to get back to reality. Cups of tea, not hot sex. 'How do you take your tea?'

'The same as I do at work every day.' He grinned. 'Milk, no sugar.'

'Sweet enough?'

'Of course.' He stood up and came around the counter. Taking her in his arms, he became serious. 'Forget the tea. We've got unfinished business to deal with.' He leaned down and kissed her gently. As a tester to see if she wanted to follow up?

Silly man. Of course she did. The only answer was to kiss him back, deeper, longer, harder. To lose all sense of being except wherever Lockie's body touched hers, where she melded with him, became a part of him. Unreal. Wonderful. She slipped her hands underneath his shirt. Her palms rubbed lightly over his warm skin and upped the temperature in her body.

Lockie's hands encased her butt, his thumbs massaging hard, then soft, then hard again. Desire flared stronger between her legs, tightened her belly, excited every part of her body. 'I want you so badly.'

He lifted her onto the bench, his head dropping to her breast. She jerked her blouse over her head.

His tongue licked her nipple through the lace of her bra.

A groan escaped her. This was unbelievable. She was alive with need. Her hands tightened around Lockie's shoulders to keep him close. Tipping her head sideways, she opened her eyes and stared around. And froze.

Lockie lifted his head. 'Caia?'

She inclined her head towards the table where McKenzie's lunchbox was. 'Not here.' No way was she going to make out with Lockie and have McKenzie walk in on them looking for something.

'Fair cop. I get it.' He lifted her up and headed to her bedroom, pausing only so she could close McKenzie's door. In her room, she flipped the lock before discarding her pants to stand before Lockie, ready for anything.

He hurriedly shucked out of his clothes And was he ready or what? Hard, large, ready to go.

Reaching for him, she held his erection and rubbed up and down slowly, savouring the sexy sensations she got from touching him. He was wonderful. More than wonderful. Amazing. Exciting.

'Wait, Caia. Slowly does it. I want to take time getting to know you this way. And for you to do the same with me.'

'Bring it on.' If she was capable of going slow. But she'd give it her all to do so. She tugged him onto the bed, and muffled an excited cry as he covered her with that body she'd been drooling about for weeks.

As they touched and kissed each other's bodies, she let go completely, drowning in the need that kept peaking, then slowing only enough for her to be able to take more touches from Lockie's tongue on her nipples. He licked a line down to her stomach, and down further until he licked her heat spot. Then there was no slowing down. Her hips lifted in anticipation as she took him in her hand and slid up and down his erection, tightening him and making her own need grow more than she'd have thought possible.

Lockie moved over her and pushed in deep, filling her with wonder.

Her muscles tightened around him, her world imploded, and she knew nothing but warmth and exhilaration when Lockie shuddered inside her. Un-be-liev-able.

Lockie curled up behind Caia, holding her close. His heart rate was slowly returning to normal, but his mind was a mess of wonder and longing. Longing for more. More moments like they'd just shared and more hours together being who they were. Two people who'd been dealt some bad cards in life and wanted a happy future.

He was presuming Caia wanted that but could have been wrong. He'd seen how different she was with her friends, how trusting and accepting of them. He'd noted caution rise when she was with people she didn't know well. More than that, she tended to back off from him when they were getting too close, as if she had no intention of giving her heart away. That he understood, but since meeting Caia, his thinking was changing and opening up to possibilities of trust and love.

Tonight Caia hadn't held back for a moment, though he'd thought she was about to when she froze in the kitchen. Fortunately her motherly instincts had stepped in and diverted them from making a huge mistake. If McKenzie had walked in on them having sex, there'd have been endless repercussions. And probably the end of whatever they'd started. He believed they had taken a step further in their relationship, getting in deeper and opening up more to each other.

'Lockie? What's wrong?'

'Not a thing.' He brushed a kiss on the back of her neck. 'How could there be? You're amazing.'

She twisted her head to look at him. He felt a surge of deep warmth at the sight of her lopsided, happier-than-he'd-ever-seen smile. 'That makes two of us.'

He'd made her happy. Which made him happy. To be responsible for that smile was special. He hadn't had sex with Caia. He'd made love to her. Bloody hell. Where did that come from? Love had nothing to do with the sex they'd shared. Even if he was starting to feel more than friendship for Caia, he was not falling in love with her. He wasn't ready. Though there had been moments when he'd felt something akin to love for Caia, it wasn't really happening.

The smile disappeared. 'You sure nothing's wrong? You look worried.'

Caia didn't let him get away with anything. He sat up and moved to the side of the bed, away from that compelling body. Despite the goings-on in his head, the rest of his body was already stirring, waking up for more excitement. Sex. Yes, better to call it sex. *Making love* was too serious. Too deep. 'Not at all. I'm still getting around the fact I'm here in your bed after having out-of-this-world sex with you.'

'Right. So not worried, just looking as if you are.' Sarcasm dripped off her tongue. 'If you think you've made a mistake being with me, then say so.'

Go for his throat, why didn't she? 'It wasn't a mistake, Caia. It was wonderful, and I'd like more. I'm also wary of overstepping the line when we've only started to get to know each other.'

'Some people know where they're at from the

moment they meet. I'm not saying you should be there yet, because I'm not. But you knocked on my door because you wanted to follow up on what we started on Sunday night. Either I wasn't as exciting as you'd hoped I'd be, or you're not telling me something.' She leaned over the side of the bed and picked up her blouse to pull it on.

'Was Garth the only one to hurt you?' He had to ask. He needed to know all he could so he might understand Caia better. After Marg, he didn't trust himself to accept an explanation without digging for more problems. It was how he was these days.

Her mouth flattened. 'My father as well. I don't want to think you'd let me down like they did, but you're avoiding telling me why you look worried.'

She was right. Okay, here it was. 'Like you, I've been hurt by someone I loved, and so I am probably OTT about looking out for myself when it comes to women. I'm not saying that because we've had sex, I'm out of here, never to spend time with you again.' He paused, gathered himself together. He had to be honest or he might as well walk away now. 'I'd like to spend more time with you, go on dates and get to know more about what makes you tick. That's if you'll put up with me.' So much for calling it a day.

She wouldn't understand how open he was being when normally he never mentioned his broken heart or how he was careful about letting go of the restraints he'd put on himself. It made him vulnerable, and that was something he'd sworn never to be again after Marg left him like she did.

Caia was taking her time answering, which was a concern. He didn't want to be dumped now. She meant a lot to him, even if he denied he was falling in love with her. As he looked at her, his heart sighed. Her hair was messed up and gorgeous. Her skin was still pink from having sex. How could he walk away? Right now it didn't seem possible, but if she told him to, he'd have no choice. Or he could get down on bended knee and beg for another chance.

'Lockie.' She smiled. 'Of course I'll put up with you. One date at a time.'

The tension eased out of his body, and he reached to hug her. 'You're wonderful.' He couldn't believe how much he meant it. She was beyond wonderful, which again was scary. But this time, he'd wait out the worry and continue the good side of whatever it was they had going between them.

Turning in his arms, Caia kissed him. 'I hate to say this, but you can't stay the night.'

'McKenzie. I get it.'

Relief flickered in her face. 'Thank you.' Then she grinned. 'Don't know why I'm thanking you when I'd like nothing more than to curl up with you for the rest of the night. Maybe have more sexercise.'

He laughed. That's how good she made him

feel. 'There'll be more, I promise. But I'd better head away or I might not leave in time.'

Caia nodded. 'McKenzie will be up early as she's excited about sports day tomorrow. She'll be wanting her lunch packed before breakfast and to be taken to school early in case she misses out on something.'

'The joys of parenthood.'

'Yep, and I wouldn't change a thing.'

A timely reminder of what was important. Lockie pulled on his shoes, kissed Caia once more just because he could and headed away with a bounce in his step.

CHAPTER NINE

'CHIN UP, EYES FORWARD,' Caia muttered as she headed inside the GP clinic. Last night was not the end of the world. Far from it. More like the beginning of something so special she had to keep pinching herself to make sure she hadn't been dreaming. The sex had been beyond amazing. Like so many things about Lockie. Now they'd been intimate, and there was no going back from that.

Hopefully he'd be as comfortable to work with today as he had been since she started and wouldn't give her the cold shoulder. He'd gone off the boil after they'd made love—had sex—and despite explaining how he felt, she still wondered if he'd changed his mind now he'd had the night to think about it.

She had no regrets, other than it was getting harder to stay in control of her feelings. Whether she was ready or not, Lockie was making his way into her heart. Being pushed faster than she wanted could be good in that she'd move past her fears quicker and become comfortable about what her heart was telling her. Or she could do a U-turn and walk away, possibly losing the opportunity to have that wonderful life she'd dreamed about.

'Morning, Caia. Coffee's on.' The man in her head walked past as she dumped her bag in her room. He sounded friendly enough.

'Thanks.' Glancing in the mirror beside a cupboard, she shrugged. Shadows underlined her eyes, and her hair was drab despite the effort she'd put into brushing it. No hiding she'd had a sleepless night.

Her phone interrupted her thoughts. 'Morning, Caia Johnstone speaking.'

'Caia, it's Tami. You helped that day when I came to see a nurse with problems relating to my pregnancy.'

'Hi, Tami. How's things?' Something wrong?

'I was discharged from hospital two days after you sent me there. Everything was good, and I've been very careful not to overdo anything.'

'But?'

'I woke up this morning with similar pains as that time, only they're sharper.'

'Where are you?'

'At Mum's.'

'Give me the address, and I'll come around now.' She'd give Tami a thorough examination, but the chances were she'd be going back to hospital. Pre-eclampsia didn't disappear overnight.

Address in hand and her kit slung over her shoulder, Caia popped into the break room to fill her coffee flask. Coffee would help her deal with rush hour traffic on the way.

'Why are you in a hurry, Caia?' Lockie strolled in behind her looking very relaxed, and nothing like the man she'd had sex with last night.

'I've had a call from Tami. Sounds like either the pre-eclampsia has returned or she's in early labour.'

'Okay, you go find out exactly what's going on.' Lockie grimaced. 'Keep me posted, will you? She's my patient too.'

'Will do.' She was out of here. Keeping Tami waiting any longer than she had to wasn't on. Nor was trying to breathe normally in the same room as Lockie. This new state of apprehension was quite exciting when she didn't overthink what could go wrong. 'See you later.'

'Caia, wait.' So much for leaving Lockie. He was right behind her as she strode across the car park.

'I can't. I need to get on the road.'

'Don't drive too fast, all right? Look out for yourself first.'

That was not what she'd expected. Once again he'd surprised her, and pushed her wonder buttons. 'Promise.' Then she spun around. 'Last night was awesome.' She hadn't planned on saying anything about their time in her bedroom, but the words spilled out and were genuine.

He reached over and lifted a wayward lock of hair away from her cheek. 'I can't argue with that.'

Smiling, she opened her car and put her pack inside. 'See you later.' She got behind the wheel and drove away, keeping one eye on the rear-vision mirror until Lockie disappeared from view. What a man.

Her phone pinged as a text came in. She waited impatiently until she had to stop for traffic lights before taking a look.

Lockie. Feel like a repeat tonight?

Toot, toot.

The light had changed to green. Tempting as it was to stay put and reply, she drove off, and then cursed when the next two sets of lights were green. Someone, something, was playing with her.

The moment she came to a stop at the next red light, she answered Lockie.

Absolutely. Come around after McKenzie's in bed, about seven, after stories are over.

They could've had this conversation when she got back to the practise, but it was fun texting. Showed how boring her love life had become.

What love life? There hadn't been one for so long, she'd almost forgotten what was involved. Apart from getting hot and sexy, and going on a date. And— 'Stop, Caia. You're getting carried away.' Too right she was, but when had she had so much fun? But it was not a love life. Not yet.

'Which pharmacy do you want me to send your prescription through to, Jeremy?' Lockie asked his patient who'd presented with a chest infection.

'The one at the mall will do.'

He clicked away on the keyboard. 'Done. I've also sent the request for blood tests to the lab, and marked them urgent so you can turn up without an appointment.'

Jeremy dragged himself upright. 'I'll go there now.'

He was usually a fit man. It was odd to see him so knocked about. 'Take it easy for the rest of the week or you won't be back on the road soon.' He regularly drove long-haul trucks up and down the North Island.

'Knew you'd say that. Partly why I didn't come in sooner.'

'Now you're paying the price.' Lockie liked the guy. He was always blunt and didn't like wasting time. But sometimes a person had to listen to their body.

Jeremy's smile was wry. 'Fair cop. Should've listened to the wife.'

He understood why Jeremy might've ignored his wife. She had a reputation for ordering her husband and children around. From what Lockie had heard, not one of them took a lot of notice of her, yet they all got on well. Who knew what made a marriage work? What kept the kids onside? One day he'd like to find out for himself.

Opening the door for Jeremy, he heard Caia talking to Annie. She was back, so everything must have gone well with Tami.

'How's Tami?' he asked when he walked in behind the reception desk. She hadn't rung him as he'd asked, but she hadn't been away long either.

'In early-stage labour. I've dropped her and her mother at the maternity hospital and will return to her once I've seen two patients here. A nurse is with her and will call if anything changes in that time, but I think it's going to be a long, slow labour.'

He locked his eyes with hers. 'All day?'

'Probably well into the night.' Her disappointment resonated between them. 'Nothing I can do but wait and see.'

A similar emotion caught at him, but he managed a big smile to show it was fine. 'Nothing to be done but go with the flow.'

She laughed. 'Not that babies flow out—not too much, anyway.'

He turned away before he said something that would have Annie catching on about how he and Caia were more than workmates. As far as he knew, apart from his partners, no one had twigged to the heat running between him and Caia, and he wanted to keep it that way. They didn't need the sideways glances and cheeky smiles. Looking at the waiting patients, he called, 'Connor, come through.'

As the teen hobbled after him on crutches, Lockie tried to ignore the need rolling through him created when standing by Caia. She did it as easily as clicking her fingers. Did she know how much she disturbed him? He hoped not or she'd have the upper hand, something he wasn't used to and wasn't keen on.

So much for hoping they'd have sex tonight. A patient had got in the way of that. Again. For the first time, he wished he could make it happen so she could have the night to do as she pleased. Probably that'd be seeing a new baby into the world. They were getting on brilliantly, but she never hesitated to shove him aside when she wanted or needed to. Because she didn't like him as much as he did her? She had a valid reason for doing so now, but would she push him away just as easily for any other reason too? He didn't want to be used, or left to wonder if she cared. If they were spending time together, then he had to be able to trust her not to walk away whenever she chose, at least not without explaining why first. Hard to imagine her doing that when it had been done to her, but he was no expert in understanding women's thinking. Or his own at times.

Six o'clock had been and gone. Caia had managed to grab a sandwich and cup of tea and phone Izzy to let her know she'd be late picking up McKenzie before Tami told her she thought the contractions were fiercer and coming faster.

Standing up after checking Tami's cervix and how far it had dilated, she nodded. 'You're right. Things are speeding up.'

Tami grimaced as another contraction made itself felt. She pushed down.

'Easy does it. You can't speed things up. Baby will arrive when he's ready and not a moment before.'

'Grrr. It'll be the only time he's in charge, I'm telling you that now.' Tami tried to relax, but she wasn't winning. 'The pain's horrendous.'

Her mother held her hand. 'You're doing fine, my girl.'

'I wish Tobias was here. Sorry, Mum, I love having you with me, but this is his baby too.'

'I know what you mean. Your father was having surgery to have his appendix removed when I was in labour. I called him all sorts of names I won't repeat, but it wasn't his fault. Nor was it mine,' she added with a smile. 'Listen to Caia and all will go well.'

Tempting fate here? Caia shrugged. Not likely.

So far everything was as it should be. Glancing at her watch, she swallowed her disappointment. Nine p.m. By the time this baby arrived, it would be way past time for Lockie to drop by her place. He could've stayed the night, too, as McKenzie was now staying with Izzy, but it wasn't meant to happen. Not tonight, but there were other nights ahead when they might get together. *Be positive.* They *would* get together. 'I'll top up the epidural if you like. It will help with the pain, but you have to understand that the urge to push won't change.'

Tami's eyes lit up briefly. 'Go for it. I'm a wimp, I know, but too bad. I want this over.'

'If I had a dollar for every time I heard those words, I'd have a fancy car to drive around in.' Caia double-checked the drug vial date and name, then drew it into a syringe. 'Lift your gown so I can access your back. That's it.' Moments later she dropped the syringe in a tray and put it out of the way.

'Feeling better already,' Tami said. 'You're good with a needle.'

'Not when it comes to patching my daughter's clothes after she's been practising skids on the lawn.' Caia laughed.

'Why would she do that?'

'Because she can. Get used to it. Kids love doing whatever gets a reaction out of their mums, whether it's sensible or not.' Then she added, 'You've got a bit of down time before your boy gets to that stage. Make the most of it. I'll look to see how baby's progressing.' Caia knelt down and lifted the cover away from Tami's lower body. She examined the cervix. 'I don't think baby's far off crowning.'

'The contractions feel stronger. Glad I had that second epidural. Who's that?' Tami's phone was ringing. Her face lit up. 'Tobias. Hey, honey. I wish you were here… Not yet, but Caia says not long to go… You're what?' Tears spurted from the corners of her eyes. 'Seriously? You're on your way home? I can't wait to see you. That's the best news. Give your boss a hug from me… What?' She laughed. 'I'm sure he'll understand.' A long groan took over.

Tami's mother took the phone from her grip and stepped away to talk to Tobias.

'Baby's crowning,' Caia reported.

'Did you hear that, Mum? Tell him our boy's coming out.'

'Whenever you feel the need to push, give it all you've got. It's hard, but this is it. You're nearly there.' The best part of a birth, Caia thought. It was something she never got tired of witnessing. 'That's it. And again.' She had her hands in position to hold the baby as he came out into the world. 'Again.' Then the baby's shoulders were free, and she carefully pulled him right out. 'There you go. He's here.'

Tami was lost for words when Caia placed her

son in her arms after cleaning him and cutting the umbilical cord.

The precious moments. She'd never forget the wonder of McKenzie opening her eyes and staring at her for the first time. Or the feel of her small, soft body against her breast. There were so many memories stored in her head she loved flicking through. Motherhood had its challenges, for sure, but it was the most amazing achievement she'd had. It would've been even more wonderful if she'd had a partner to share it all with, and everything that came afterwards. The downside to being a single mother, but she wouldn't have Garth back in her life even if it meant McKenzie then had a father. Not just a name on a birth certificate kind of father, but a man who'd probably hurt his daughter as he'd hurt her mother.

'I'm going to film you and the baby and send it to Tobias,' said Tami's mother.

'That's cool.' Tami was crying and smiling all at once.

'I'll give you some time alone. I'll be in the office if you need anything. Just ask someone to get me.' Caia breathed in deep. What a special moment, even if the dad wasn't here.

Waiting for the kettle to boil, she called Lockie. 'Hi. Baby's here, and Mum's over the moon. Even better, Dad's on his way home from Australia.' She was babbling, but it was always a relief when a birth went so well.

'You sound just about as thrilled as Tami must be.' Lockie laughed.

'I am.'

'Where are you now?' Something like hope came through the connection.

'At the birthing unit. It's too soon to leave Tami and baby. I'll be here for a quite while yet.' At least McKenzie was sorted, though she never liked leaving her girl with Izzy overnight. She was her mother and wanted McKenzie to understand she was always there for her. Or nearly always, but the times she wasn't, she was being a normal parent. As long as it didn't happen too often. 'Sorry, but that's how it is.'

'I'd be shocked if you did anything differently. I'm sorry I won't be seeing you tonight, but don't worry about it. I know we'll find another time. Can't get too annoyed that a new baby came into this world tonight—that would be selfish, and I don't think that's me.'

'I know it's not you. I'm also glad you seem to understand me so much you know where I'm coming from.' Blah. She did get a bit too cute with Lockie at times. She'd blame the fact she felt emotional after the birth, true or not. 'I won't be delivering babies every night of the week.'

'But I've got meetings two nights and dinner with the parents another.'

Bugger. Disappointment lodged in her chest, but she wasn't about to complain. 'That's life.'

'I'm afraid so. I'll see you at work tomorrow.'

'Will do. Good night, Lockie.'

'Good night, Caia. Sleep tight.'

Hardly likely now that Lockie had been between her sheets and she knew what it felt like to be cuddled up against his sensational body. 'I'll do my best.'

'Me, too.'

So they were on the same page. Disappointed and remembering what it had been like to make love last night. Or have sex. Whichever way they thought about it. She went with making love. Lockie had not only given her the most wonderful time sexually, but he'd also curled up against her, holding her as though she meant more than a hot date. As though he cared for her a little. She'd been comfortable with him and not wondering when he'd get out of bed and go home as she'd done a couple of times in the past with men she'd slept with to deal with the need she'd been feeling. With Lockie, it had been about getting to know him better and being able to drop her hang-ups over getting it right with a man, as well as having a good time.

It was odd how the week flew by while also dragging along so slowly Lockie thought the weekend would never come. Seeing Caia every day wound him up so tight at times he was afraid he'd explode with desire for her. That wouldn't be a good look at work with other staff seeming to be watching out for him and Caia more than usual.

While it was plain exciting, it also felt as though his pulse was on a treadmill, speeding up when she was near, slowing down when she was in her room or down the road at the midwifery facility.

'Got anything on this weekend?' Caia asked on Friday morning.

'Game of golf tomorrow followed by dinner at the clubhouse afterwards.'

The disappointment in her face stirred his guilt, but he wasn't changing his plans. These plans had been in place for weeks. He played golf with his mates on a regular basis, and he wasn't prepared to change that. If he and Caia got closer, he would, but kicking his friends to the sideline now only to find Caia wasn't becoming a part of his life further on would mean he'd upset his friends for no good reason. He was coming to believe he was ready to form a relationship, but the old fears hadn't backed off completely, so he was covering all options. Was he being selfish? Better this way than to take all he could from Caia and then have to walk away.

'You really enjoy playing golf, don't you?' She was trying to keep her disappointment in line.

'Yes, I do. Whacking the ball is a great way to relieve any tension left over from dealing with difficult cases in here. As long as I hit it properly, that is.' He was trying to lighten the unhappy mood that had descended. 'I'm not a pro by a long way.'

It worked. She smiled.

'Just damned good.'

Her smile widened. 'Of course you are.'

Give me more of those smiles and I'll do just about anything you ask. 'Have you ever had a go at golf?'

'Nope, and don't suggest I do. Why would I want to spend hours trying to get a small ball into an even smaller hole?'

'Not quite smaller, but I get the gist of what you're saying. One day I might talk you into giving it a crack just for the hell of it. Who knows? You could find you enjoy the sport.'

Caia laughed. Another plus. 'I'm not into sports of any kind. Haven't really had the time since I left high school, where I did play a bit of tennis. Wasn't terribly great at that either.'

'Either? What do you mean? You're a great midwife, an even greater mother.'

Her smile softened. 'I could get to like you.'

That was the plan. 'I'd better get back to work before someone comes looking for me.' That'd be highly unusual, but he'd been distracted lately. He was usually on top of his schedule, except when a patient needed more time than allocated because of a serious condition.

Caia stood up. 'Me too.'

Thankfully they were the only people in the break room or their conversation might've been misinterpreted, especially Caia's comment just before. A comment that softened his heart and shoved aside any concerns about getting too involved too fast. A bit late for that anyway. They were involved, and he was staying around to see where it led. Caia had got to him big time.

Friday night and McKenzie was running around the place like Lockie's childhood springer spaniel doing the zoomies. She was exhausted, and Caia was hoping she'd run out of steam sooner rather than later. From past experience, she knew there was no other way to calm her girl when she was like this.

So much for a quiet glass of wine and unwinding from the week. Her patient numbers were growing faster than expected, and everyone at the practise was pleased. Especially Caia, as she liked to be kept busy. There was only so much tidying cupboards and folding sheets she could cope with before feeling she was going stir-crazy.

The doorbell rang.

Who would that be? Not Lockie. He'd said quite pointedly that he was tied up with various commitments all week.

McKenzie spun around and charged towards the door.

'McKenzie, stop. You know you're not allowed

to open the door without me there.' She followed and caught her arm. 'Slow down.'

'Can I open it now? You're here.'

Caia peeped through the door viewer.

Lockie stood there looking wonderful. When didn't he? Thump, thump went her heart. He'd found time to drop by.

Tapping her girl on her shoulder, she grinned. 'Go on, open it.'

McKenzie twisted the knob and tugged the door wide. 'Daddy,' she shrieked loud enough for the whole street to hear as she threw herself at Lockie, wrapping her arms tight around him. 'Daddy.'

Lockie looked stunned. Then his face became blank as he gently removed McKenzie's arms from around him and stepped back. 'McKenzie, I am not your father,' he said quietly but with purpose that indicated he'd never be interested in anything more serious than a brief fling with McKenzie's mother.

Caia's stomach dropped to her toes, followed by her heart. She had leapt into the relationship too quickly, and now McKenzie was paying the price by feeling she was missing out on a dad, a feeling her mother knew all too well because of her own father. Something she'd never meant to happen to her daughter. 'Come here, sweetheart.' Grabbing McKenzie, she tugged her away from Lockie and up into her arms. 'McKenzie, sweetheart, Lockie's right. He's not your father.' He wasn't becoming a part of their lives and therefore couldn't fulfil the role of McKenzie's father. *She'd* been stupid to think she could have fun with him and not be hurt. And that McKenzie wouldn't be hurt. This had been a timely reminder to stick to her determination not to become involved with any man.

'Why not?' she shouted. 'All my friends have daddies. Why can't I?'

Caia's knees started to buckle. She understood exactly what McKenzie wanted. But she wasn't getting it. This was exactly what she'd hoped to prevent when explaining to McKenzie that Lockie was her boss and friend, nothing else. But five-year-olds didn't stop to think about what they were saying, just shouted out the words.

She slammed a hand against the wall to steady herself. It felt like a blind was coming down over her face, trying to hide the raft of emotions pouring through her, making her speechless. Devastating her. Where did that come from? Her heart was breaking for her girl. Growing up without a father was awful. She knew that. But for McKenzie to latch on to Lockie like that had tipped their worlds upside down.

'Mummy, why not?'

Lifting McKenzie up, she held her close and turned towards the lounge, hoping her legs had the strength to carry her the short distance. She had no idea what to say except repeat Lockie wasn't her daddy and was never likely to be.

Behind her, the front door snipped shut. Had he left without a word? A quick glance over her shoulder showed him looking devastated as well as thoughtful, the anger appearing to have backed off, but she knew he was still upset. At least he hadn't bolted and was following her into the lounge.

She sank onto a chair, still holding McKenzie tight. Too tight. But she was protecting her girl. And herself. Because the expression on Lockie's face didn't bode well for the coming conversation. That was if he didn't turn around and disappear from her private life. Here she'd been thinking she and Lockie might have a chance of making it work between them. Now? No way. Protecting her daughter came first, and the looks passing over Lockie's face told her he wasn't about to say he was staying around. Standing up she said, 'I'll put McKenzie to bed.'

Keeping a grip on the thoughts racing around her head, she quickly had McKenzie tucked in bed, and after closing the door she returned to face Lockie. 'I don't know where that came from. Not the bit about wanting a dad. I get that. But why she threw herself at you as though her mind was made up? She set herself up for a huge disappointment.'

Hurt filled his face. 'Thanks a bloody lot, Caia.'

'Well, it's true.'

Lockie turned to stare out the window. What the hell had just gone down? One moment he'd been pressing the doorbell, happy to be seeing Caia. The next he'd been upended by a five-year-old tornado breaking his heart, and waking him up to the real consequences of spending time with Caia. Who sounded like she was blaming him for what happened.

He'd just learned he was *not* ready for a full-on relationship and all it involved.

'You think I accept McKenzie calling you daddy? When we haven't had a relationship other than a couple of dates and one night in my bed? Do you?' While he struggled to find the answer to her questions, she continued. 'Well, here it is. I have a daughter. She comes first in my life. So if you think she won't matter in a relationship with me, think again. Her father didn't want to know her, and I won't have another man letting her down.'

He snapped. 'Caia, not once have I said or done a thing to suggest McKenzie is not part of you and your life.'

She was staring at him as though he had two heads.

Which right now it felt a little like he did. He'd thought they were getting somewhere with their relationship. Now he wondered if Caia had felt anything for him at all or if she was using him for some fun and nothing else.

'Go on,' she growled.

What was she expecting him to say? Damn it. Within seconds everything had changed between them, and somehow he doubted there'd ever be a chance of righting the mess. Did he want to? He had no answer. 'I have enjoyed the time we've spent together and believed we'd continue sharing some more fun moments.' But now he was remembering how he'd loved the wonderful years with Marg, the love and all that involved, and how she held back from him so much about what she was thinking and going through. Already the fences were going up, keeping Caia on the outside. He wasn't letting her in. The guilt he'd carried over not seeing what Marg had been going through had been huge. Surely he wasn't doing that again? He knew Caia was holding back from telling him more than the fact that she'd been let down by the two most important men in her life. Could he let her in and help her get over what those men did while risking his heart too? But he couldn't face it all going wrong and leaving him broken again.

He was vulnerable.

She was vulnerable.

McKenzie too.

'McKenzie came up with that word with no

input from me,' he said softly around the sudden lump in his throat.

'I know.' Tears were flooding Caia's face.

It was hard not to take both of them in his arms and hold them until the storm passed. But if he did, then he'd have committed himself to forever. He was not going down that path. He'd had a timely reminder about how easy it was to get hurt, and he wasn't going there. Not for anyone. He wasn't ready and now doubted he would ever be. He'd been fooling himself thinking he might have found the woman he could love. 'We're lucky we didn't get too involved before this happened or it could've had bigger consequences for the little one.'

'I understand what you're saying, and I'm not blaming you for what happened. The thing is, I can't continue with what we've started. McKenzie's not going to get over you popping around here in a matter of hours or even days, Lockie. Believe me when I say I know how she feels. It sucks missing out on a parent. All I can do is set an example by being strong and hope she copes.'

'You do that very well,' he told her quietly. Because it was true. There was so much to this amazing woman he didn't fully understand. There was a lot to her story he still didn't know and wasn't going to find out now. To stay would only set them all up for more pain, because he was not getting involved full-time. Not at all. The pain was already knocking at him, bringing up the memories he'd worked so hard to bury over the years since Marg died. The only person who could protect him was himself. And he wasn't doing a very good job of it.

'I'd like you to go.' Caia was staring at him with disappointment reflected in those beautiful green eyes. 'Now.'

'I'd like to—'

'Go. Now.'

'Tell you you're a wonderful woman, Caia, and I wish you everything you want for the future.'

She bent over her daughter, her chin resting on McKenzie's head.

The silence was deafening as he headed for the door and let himself out into a chilly night. He'd been saved from heartbreak by a little girl who only wanted to be loved. He was walking away to save her heart along with his. As for her mother, he was going to miss her for a long time to come. Seeing her at work would make day-to-day normality difficult, if not near impossible, but he'd make it happen. It had to for both their sakes. Even more difficult would be not being dropping in to see Caia at home, where she was much more relaxed.

He was hurting. A lot, though it could've been worse if they'd continued seeing each other. How much worse? His heart was in pieces. His head was spinning. As for his dreams of the future, they'd gone up in a ball of smoke. He hadn't realised how far he'd fallen for Caia. Perhaps he should be thanking McKenzie. Except that didn't fit comfortably. His world had fallen apart over one word.

Daddy.

A simple word. An equally complex one. One that had struck him at the core of who he believed he was. He'd known that some day he'd like to be a father. He just hadn't realised how much he wanted that. But it didn't mean he was letting McKenzie sway him. She was delightful, and yet he and Caia weren't ready for anything near as deep and meaningful as him stepping into McKenzie's life permanently. What's more, Caia had been abundantly clear where she stood, and that was not with him. She was protecting her girl. As she should.

So was he, her realised. As well as himself. It should feel good, but it didn't. He'd made a huge mistake somewhere along the way with Caia. He'd let her in, and now he had to push her away again. He wasn't ready. Would probably never be. But if he ever was, he had to consider Caia before himself. She didn't need her world tipped upside down again because of him. If only there was a way to make things easier for all of them.

He pulled away from Caia's home without a glance. There was already too much thumping going on behind his ribs to add to the turmoil she'd caused. He was looking ahead, going forward with life as it used to be a few weeks ago when he wasn't intrigued and then half in love with her. He'd run solo for a long time. He could do it again when this time there was less to lose. Dreams, not reality.

CHAPTER TEN

'GET READY FOR your swimming lesson, McKenzie.' Caia slopped around the house in baggy denim shorts and a T-shirt. Hopefully taking her girl to the pool would distract her overwrought mind for a while.

McKenzie stamped her foot and shouted, 'I don't want to go.'

'Do not talk to me like that, missy, or you'll have to fold the washing when we get home.' Hard as it was, Caia held back from hauling her into her arms to give her a hug. McKenzie would only think she could shout again.

'Don't care.' There were shadows under McKenzie's eyes from lack of sleep. During the night, she'd crawled into bed with her mum, asking why she couldn't have a daddy.

Holding McKenzie close, Caia had stumbled through an explanation, telling her that it wasn't her fault she didn't have a father, and not all children had one living with them. She wanted to say that one day they might if Mum met someone special, but that would only raise her girl's hopes and inflict more pain when it didn't happen.

She did owe McKenzie for screwing up over her father. Telling a five-year-old that her real father had left them before she was born wasn't easy, but the time had come to be honest. She'd been brief with the details, and McKenzie had plenty of questions. McKenzie seemed to accept what Caia told her, but Caia wasn't so sure she was finished with the subject. One day at a time was the only way she knew how to deal with this. Caia was thankful Lockie hadn't been mentioned again.

He'd been quick to back off when McKenzie called him daddy. She couldn't blame him for his reaction. He'd been as shocked as she'd been. At least he hadn't tried to tell her she was wrong to say they were over, taking her heart with him. Instead he'd seemed keen to get away. So far he hadn't shown he was prepared to talk about something important. Just like Garth, who'd always been a talkative man. She seemed to have made the same mistake with Lockie, believing because he talked quite a lot and always appeared relaxed that he wouldn't hold back on anything important. A wake-up call she was thankful for because she could adjust to reality and stop living in a dream. Except her heart was closing in on itself, and she was hurting. She loved Lockie. No denying it.

'Come on, sweetheart. After swimming, we'll

get some chips and chicken for lunch.' She wasn't above spoiling her when necessary.

'Can I wear my new swimsuit?' The one she hadn't been allowed to wear last week because she'd thrown a tantrum about wanting to change it for another colour after she'd worn it in the pool the week before.

'Yes.' Anything for peace. There was enough distress going on in her head without McKenzie adding to it. After swimming, she was having Jessie and Jodie for the weekend while Izzy and Brett went to a wedding at a vineyard where they had overnight accommodation. At least she'd be kept busy and hopefully distracted from Lockie and what might've been if they'd continued getting to know each other better. More sex had been on the menu. Probably just as well that wasn't happening as he was very distracting when he was touching her all over, and she forgot about remaining cautious. In fact, she owed her girl for forcing her to take a reality check. She and Lockie were not getting into a relationship of any kind. His trust issues appeared as deep as hers, which would not be helpful when it came to feeling safe with him.

'Cool, Mummy.'

A sad sigh trickled over her lips. She was back in the good books with her girl. If only it was that simple to fix the fallout between her and Lockie. The moment had been short and blunt, but truthful—on her part, anyway. Hurt had been there too. The last thing she'd ever wanted to hear was Lockie saying he wished her everything she wanted for the future before he turned and walked away. It felt permanent.

It was Lockie she wanted. He was wonderful. It was too easy to give herself to him in many ways. As much as she had to protect herself and McKenzie right now, she was struggling to accept he was gone out of her life other than as a colleague. And where work was concerned, she was stuck with the rock and hard place issue. She couldn't chuck her job in. She needed the income and to be doing what she loved. Going out on her own wasn't a serious option. There'd be too many days with not a lot happening until she was up and running properly. Anyway, she preferred working with other people around. It was a lot less lonely to have medically savvy people on hand to discuss cases with when something was going wrong.

'Tada.' McKenzie bounced into the room, arms akimbo and legs wide as she showed off her swimsuit. 'It's pretty.'

'It is, and so are you, sweetheart. Right, let's get on the way.' Then she'd have other things to focus on and not the pain in her chest.

Monday morning, Caia pulled into the staff parking lot and grabbed her bag before she gave in and headed back home and phoned in sick. She could do this. Had to. There was no point in hiding for a day or two, because nothing would change. She and Lockie had issues, but for the life of her, she was not letting them interfere with her job.

Slamming the door closed, she strode inside the practise building. Bring it on. There was a staff meeting to start the day off, and she'd get a feel for how Lockie was going to handle this while making him aware she wasn't walking away from her position because they didn't see eye to eye on what had started out as fun and turned to hell.

'Morning, Caia.'

Her grip tightened on her bag. 'Morning, Lockie. Did you win your golf match?'

He held the door open for her. ''Fraid not.'

So far all was good. No smiles coming her way, but she hadn't found one for him either. 'Need more practise?'

'Probably. How was your weekend?' He sounded offhand.

'Good. Swimming lessons on Saturday, and Izzy's girls stayed overnight.'

'So you were busy.' He closed the door and turned towards his room.

She turned the other way towards her room. 'I certainly was.' She wouldn't have had time for a date if he'd asked. Which he hadn't. They were done. Thankfully he was talking to her without ice in his voice. Not a lot of warmth either, but better than she'd expected.

Which was good when everyone was sitting around the tearoom table, coffees and teas in hand as the weekly meeting got under way. It was hard not to look at Lockie sitting opposite her and recall those special moments they'd shared. And how broken she felt now they were finished. He was mesmerising when she didn't think about protecting her heart. He could make her life into a dream, or he could wreck it completely. *Daddy.* That one word had wrenched her heart and wised her up. She had fallen for Lockie, but the moment that word flew out of McKenzie's mouth, the barriers had gone back in place. She could blame Lockie for not caring as much as she'd hoped, but she had been quick to say they were over. She hadn't even thought it through. She'd made her own decisions and stuck by them.

'Caia? You with us?' Katie asked.

Shaking her head clear of Lockie, she found a smile. 'I'm here.'

'Bring us up to date with patients. Numbers and how far into their pregnancies.'

Gathering her thoughts and focusing on what was required, she rattled off the data without looking at her laptop, finishing up with, 'I'm seeing two new patients today as well.'

'You're doing well. The numbers are better

than we'd budgeted on for the first two months,' Dave said.

'I think that's because women have been desperate for a midwifery unit in their area. It's a no-brainer to sign up now they've got one.' She wasn't taking credit for something she'd had nothing to do with. She was the midwife, not a salesperson rounding up customers.

'You might be right, but word's out that you are good at what you do,' Dave commented.

Lockie was being unusually quiet.

'Glad to hear it.' Her stomach tightened despite Dave's compliment. She glanced at Lockie and got a nod back. So he agreed with his partners. Another sigh, this one loosening the tension holding her still. Somehow they'd move on and remain colleagues, at least.

The receptionist came through the door. 'Caia, Karen Kellerman phoned to say she's bleeding and is on her way here with her mother.'

'Let me know the moment she arrives.'

'She's five months pregnant? Or is it six?' Lockie had his doctor's hat on.

'Six. Second trimester, so it doesn't sound good.' She stood up. 'If you don't mind, everyone, I'll go and get prepared.' There wasn't much to do, but preparing made caia feel calmer. The bed had clean linen and all the equipment she might need was at hand, but going through Karen's file so she knew exactly where they were at would suffice.

'Go for it.' Lockie again. 'Come and get me if there are any problems.'

Another knot loosened in her belly. 'Will do.'

An hour later, Caia stood outside watching the ambulance pull out of the car park with Karen on board and her mother following in her car, feeling devastated for the young girl. She'd accepted her pregnancy and had even started looking forward to being a mother, and now that wasn't going to happen. She'd miscarried shortly after arriving at the clinic and was going to hospital for further treatment.

Lockie had overseen the miscarriage with her and was now back in his room getting on with his patients.

She needed to do the same. There was a house call to make before she met the two new patients. Nothing like having plenty to do to keep her mind busy and off the subject of Lockie.

Caia had everything under control, including her attitude towards him, thought Lockie. While he'd been concerned she'd make it awkward to be around her, she'd been the complete opposite. Something he was grateful for. He hoped he was coming across just as well.

None of which made it any easier being in the same building as Caia. He'd missed her all weekend, had come close to going around to apologise for walking away. Except he believed he'd done the right thing. He didn't want to hurt Caia, and this was the only way he knew to avoid that. And yes, he was also protecting himself. The thought of being hurt again made him recoil and go find something else to fill in his time. He wasn't ready to fall in love. It was too risky.

It hadn't helped when his father had a crack at him at dinner on Saturday night about spending too much time working and not enough on getting out there and having a social life. Harry had copped it as well. They'd decided later when away from the parents that what was really wanted here were some grandchildren. Which had irked him because immediately McKenzie came to mind.

Daddy.

He and Caia hadn't been deep enough into a relationship that he could act as though he was filling the father role. Anyway, making the decision to stay away from Caia didn't come down to McKenzie. That was due to his heart not being ready to take a risk on Caia.

'Hey, Doc, how're you doing?'

'Good, thanks, Jerry.' His next patient had arrived. Knowing he'd get a long-winded answer, he steeled himself to ask, 'how about you?'

'Not bad.'

That was to the point. Unusual. 'Take a seat. See you're due for a prescription renewal. Is that why you're here?'

'That and because I can't sleep for more than an hour at a time.'

Something he could relate to. 'Are you worrying about anything?' Caia followed him into bed. She hung around all night so that every time he opened his eyes, he was looking for the real deal, not the image behind his eyelids.

'Just the usual day-to-day rubbish.'

Concentrate. Right now sorting Jerry's sleep deprivation was more important than the cause of his own. 'Shove your sleeve up so I can take your blood pressure.'

On Friday morning, Lockie dropped his pen on his desk and stood up to stretch his back. It had been one hell of a long week with the afternoon still to get through before he headed home and got the lawnmower out. Lunchtime had finally arrived. He wasn't overly hungry, but a walk in the fresh air might clear his head while keeping him out of the break room until Caia had finished her lunch. He'd heard her talking to Katie as they walked past his open door heading that way. She sounded chipper, though when he'd checked her out earlier, he could see she was exhausted. He suspected falling out with him might be the cause. He could have been wrong, but he believed she'd been enjoying their time together, especially that night in her bedroom.

So much for a repeat. That idea came to an end

in a blaze of emotions. Better sooner than later, when he might've been more involved with Caia. Who was he kidding? He'd already reached the point where he wanted to know all there was to know about her, and to share more of himself. Though he was still wary of opening up completely. That might take a lot longer. The problem there was that he couldn't deny the emotions Caia was evoking within him. Emotions he hadn't known for a long time. Good, warm emotions he'd hoped to find again one day. Yet now he had, he'd backed off in one hell of a hurry. What was wrong with him? Had Marg really screwed with him so much that he wouldn't expose his fears and try again? Or was he being OTT and needed to get over himself?

'I'm going next door to the bakery. Want anything?' Dave stood in the doorway.

Food. He needed to eat but couldn't get enthusiastic. Damn it. 'I'll come with you and see what they've got.'

'No different to every other day, I'd say. You look like you could do with some sleep, mate.'

'Bit early in the day for that,' he quipped. Then felt bad. Dave was watching out for him. 'I wouldn't mind a whole night out for the count.'

'What's bothering you?'

Lots of things. 'Caia.' Her name was out before he thought about it.

'Figured. She's looking worse for wear too.'

'You're too astute for my liking.'

Dave laughed. 'Good. Word of advice. Talk. Whatever the problem, talk to her about it. That's all I'm saying.'

'Thank goodness for that.' Dave had a point though. Talking things through was the only way out the other end without feeling as though he hadn't tried hard enough. What to say, though? *Hey, I'm sorry I baulked when McKenzie called me daddy, but I don't intend falling in love with you, so figured I'd better put space between us.* Straight to the point was never a bad way to go, except there was a lot missing from that statement. Things like *I'm scared because I'm falling for you, anyway.* Then there was *I don't know how to trust anymore, but I want you to trust me.*

'What you getting?' Dave interrupted his private conversation.

As he stared at the food cabinet, nothing appealed, but he needed to eat. 'Seafood roll and a Chelsea bun,' he told the woman behind the counter and delved into his pocket for his card.

As they wandered back to the practise, he asked Dave, 'What've you got planned for the weekend?'

'Watching Jordan play his final game of soccer for the season, planting out the vegetable garden, and taking it easy.'

'Sounds ideal.' Family life. If only he had that.

He could if he had the balls to give it a go. 'I've got a game of golf tomorrow.'

Caia swallowed two paracetamol tablets. This must have been the longest week in her life. One of them, anyway. Now the weekend was upon her, she could unwind from the tension caused by working around Lockie. It was as though someone was playing games with her. She'd seen more of Lockie at the clinic than in the previous weeks since she began working for the practise. As hard as she'd tried to keep everything running smoothly, she was shattered and needed nothing more than some space at home with McKenzie doing very little.

'Time for a coffee break,' Val stood in the doorway. 'You got any spare ones?' She nodded at the paracetamol packet. 'My hip's giving me grief.'

'Here, help yourself.' She handed a sachet of ten tablets over. 'Keep the rest.'

'Thanks. I forgot to pick up my prescription. So much for taking the dog for a walk along the beach this morning. He wouldn't stop heading into the water and dragging me with him.'

'Sounds harder than teaching a five-year-old that she has to go to school regardless of what she thinks.' McKenzie had thrown a paddy that morning, refusing to get dressed until Caia put her in the car in her pyjamas, telling her she was going to school like that. The stunned expression on her little face gave Caia the response she'd been looking for. It was funny now, but at the time, it'd been another hassle she didn't need.

'I remember those days.' Val laughed. 'It doesn't get any easier either.'

'Just what I need to hear.' In the break room, Caia hesitated at the sight of Lockie standing, hands on those sexy hips as he stared out the window. Damn it. She couldn't even have a coffee without bumping into him. Would he notice if she disappeared?

'What's so fascinating, Lockie?' Val asked.

He turned slowly, obviously unhappy at being interrupted in whatever he was thinking. 'Checking the weather as I'm playing in a golf tournament tomorrow.' He was looking directly at her.

Telling her what? Not to expect him to turn up at her place? She had no doubt about that, golf or not. They were over. Ignoring him, she poured two coffees and handed one to Val. 'There you go. Take some weight off the hip for a while.'

'There's some shortbread in the tin on the shelf. Help yourselves,' Lockie said. 'Murray's wife brought it in earlier as a thank-you for saving him.'

Caia shuddered. The guy had a cardiac arrest right in front of the reception desk on Tuesday, only forty-five and apparently fit. It had been a shock to everyone. Went to show no one knew what was around the corner. 'That's lovely of her. Especially when she's no doubt stressed to the max.'

'It might be her way of diverting her focus for a little while,' Lockie said. 'What are you up to this weekend?'

None of your business. But she had to play the friends game around here. 'Swimming lessons for McKenzie and not a lot else planned.' Sounded pathetic. 'That doesn't mean we won't be flat-out doing stuff.'

'I'm sure.' He sounded like he meant it, but then, he did know she didn't go out a lot other than to spend time with Izzy. 'I'd better get on with things. Have a great weekend, ladies.'

'What's up with him?' Val wondered out loud. 'He's been morose all week.'

'No idea.' Caia bit into a piece of shortbread. 'Yum. That lady can make this for us any day of the week.' It was delicious. More importantly, she needed a change of subject. Talking about Lockie was not happening. 'I'm going to try making some.' That'd fill in an hour, and might even turn out to be tasty.

If only they hadn't fallen out. It might be fun to go and watch Lockie swing a golf club at the tournament. To see those arms flex their muscles. To watch him concentrate on the ball. To think how that firm body had felt against hers as they made love. *No, we didn't. We had sex.* Making love came full of promise for the future, for more than a quickie between the sheets. Making love meant giving her heart to him, and she was not ready to do that. Not after that shocked look on his face. The look that said he had no intention of getting so involved with her that he'd have to take McKenzie into account as well. She owed McKenzie for that. She'd seen the reality behind his actions and knew they weren't going any further.

While her heart ached for him, she knew she had done the right thing. She was never going to be hurt again.

Lockie automatically popped bread into the toaster and filled the kettle as he stared out the window. The sky was bright blue, and not a hint of a breeze ruffled the leaves on the trees. A perfect day for golf.

Except he wasn't in the mood. As in big-time not interested in hitting a ball around the green.

He hadn't gone to bed last night. Instead, he'd sat in his recliner and pondered his navel.

Caia had been in his mind all the time, as she had been since last weekend, when he'd walked away from her.

He hadn't been honest with her, in that he hadn't told her why he was afraid to love and trust. If he didn't talk to her about his past, then he was going to be forever stuck in this groove, longing for Caia and afraid to give her a chance to show him her heart. He'd seen how loving she was to those who were special to her. On one level, he knew that if she fell in love with him, she'd be just as staunch with him as those special people. On another, he struggled to accept that she could give him so much because he wasn't good enough for her. Chances were he'd eventually let her down as he had Marg. After all, he'd been quick to walk away the other night. He'd struggled with being emotionally available with Marg, and now he was doing the same with Caia.

She'd told him her father and the father of her daughter had left her, and her mother hadn't been close, but nothing else. Wasn't that more than enough? Of course it was. It was more than he'd told her about Marg. Another thought occurred to him. How had those two men made her feel? Her mother? Did she blame herself? Or believe she wasn't worthy of love? She certainly pushed him away anytime he tried do anything for her.

There was only one way to learn the answers, but was he prepared to front up and ask Caia? Was he ready to expose himself and his fears completely? He needed to be. Caia was more than worthy or love. She deserved it all, love and care and happiness. And he had plenty to give her.

As he slathered butter on the overcooked toast, a truth hit hard enough to hurt his chest. His heart. He did not want to continue living the way he did at the moment. He wanted to open up and show his true feelings and stop holding back. He truly wanted to pick up those dreams he used to have and run with them wherever they led. More than that, there was only one person he could think of sharing them with. Caia.

'Goodness, McKenzie loves being in the water.' Izzy grinned. 'Even more than my two, and that's saying something.'

'Yet she didn't want to come this morning.' Caia sighed. They were sitting on seats overlooking the pool where McKenzie was having her lesson, and where, at the far end, Izzy's girls were playing and splashing around like springer spaniels. 'I don't know what's going on with her. She's quite moody at the moment.' But she did have a good idea what the problem was. McKenzie wanted a father.

'Like her mum.'

'Thanks, pal.' But Izzy was right. She had been down in the dumps all week, and so far today, nothing was improving. But she wasn't changing anything just to make her daughter happy.

'You going to tell me what's going on? I'm presuming you and Lockie aren't seeing eye to eye at the moment.'

Another sigh. They were becoming too frequent. 'Nope.'

'Then you'd better not look around behind us.'

'What?' Caia jerked around and instantly

locked eyes with Lockie. 'What the hell's he doing here?'

'Go ask him.'

Caia turned back to watch McKenzie, hunkering down as her heart pounded and her head spun. 'No.' She didn't want to talk to Lockie. They'd only fall out about something else, and that was the last thing she needed when she was trying to move on from what they'd briefly shared.

Lockie appeared in her vision. 'Hello, Caia. Izzy.'

So much for avoiding him, but he had to be here to see her and wouldn't go away until he had. 'Lockie.' Hang on. 'Aren't you meant to be playing in a golf tournament?'

'I pulled out. Have other things on my mind.'

Izzy stood up and walked further down the pool.

'Thanks, pal,' Caia repeated under her breath.

Lockie didn't take Izzy's place, instead stayed where he was, his gaze fixed on her. 'Can we go somewhere and talk?' he asked. 'Not now. I realise you want to watch McKenzie, but afterwards?'

What for? To be told he wasn't interested in long-term relationships while that was all she wanted with him? Would getting whatever was on his mind out of the way make it less awkward working together? Maybe she should tell him how much he'd let her down by walking away. Then she'd stop wasting time thinking about what might've been. 'All right. I'll see if Izzy can look after McKenzie when her lesson's finished.'

'Thank you.' Lockie turned to look at McKenzie floating on her back as the instructor talked to her. There was a softening in his stance. His shoulders lifted and fell slowly back into place, and when he turned back to Caia, caution filled his face. 'That day we met at the hospital, I was filling in time seeing a patient while waiting to donate some of my bone marrow for a child with leukaemia. I've sometimes wondered if McKenzie was the recipient.'

Her mouth dropped open. She shut it. Of all the things she'd thought he might say, that was not on the list. 'Why do you think that?'

'There were other children having transplants, but it seems a bit of a coincidence that I was donating marrow on the day McKenzie was having a transplant. More than that, it feels kind of odd that we've met again since, as if it was meant to be.'

She shivered. If it was Lockie's bone marrow McKenzie received, that was wonderful, and she'd be forever grateful to him, but it didn't change anything between them. 'I haven't looked into finding out who the donor was. It doesn't change anything for McKenzie.' But now she was starting to think *she* wanted to know and wouldn't be happy until she did. Though surely that wasn't why he'd turned up here?

'You're right.' He drew a breath. 'I've donated twice and will probably do it again, because I know what it's like when you think you're going to lose someone special due to leukaemia. Harry, my brother who's the pathologist, had acute leukaemia as a child, and a stem cell transplant saved him.'

Knock her over. Her heart pounded. She didn't know what to say, but she tried. 'You understood my outburst that day at the hospital. Now I know why.'

'I did. I was always glad I'd been there at that moment when you were beyond desperate.'

'It was the worst day of my life.'

McKenzie ran up to her, squealing, 'Mummy, did you see me floating? I can float on my back.' Then she stopped. 'Lockie, why are you here?'

'Hey, McKenzie. I came to see your mum. Is that all right?'

She shrugged. 'Whatever. Mummy, can I swim with Jessie and Jodie?'

'Yes, you can.' Glancing at Lockie she said, 'I'll check with Izzy that she's okay to have McKenzie, and I'll meet you outside.' She didn't wait for an answer, instead took her girl's hand and walked to the other end of the pool where Izzy was quick to oblige, getting her head round what Lockie had told her. It didn't change where they were, though. He was a hero for donating, but she wasn't looking for a hero, just a wonderful man at her side to go through life with.

'Give him a chance, Caia. He's a good man.'

'I know.' Suddenly it was all too obvious. He was awesome, and she loved him, so what wouldn't she do to win him over? Steady on. One thing at a time. Find out why he came to see her. If he didn't open up, then she needed to stop and think how much of a risk she was prepared to take.

Lockie was waiting for her outside the main entrance. 'Feel like going for a walk along the shoreline? Or would you prefer to go to a cafe?'

'The shoreline.' Stretching her legs while listening to whatever he'd come to tell her would be far better than stuck in a cafe surrounded by rowdy people.

For a while, they walked in silence. It wasn't uncomfortable, even though Caia couldn't stop wondering why Lockie had come to see her. She'd never thought he would. Maybe all was not lost after all.

Finally he said, 'I was married once. Marg was the love of my life. I thought it couldn't get any better. We had it all.'

Glancing sideways, she noted the determination in his chin as though he had to get this out before he changed his mind. About to say he didn't have to, she paused. Of course he did if they were going anywhere with a supposed relationship. 'Go on.'

'We'd been married three and a half years. I was in my qualifying year and working in various cities as trainee doctors do, which meant I wasn't at home a lot. Marg was a lawyer working every hour available. There was a lot of pressure on her to work hard.' Lockie paused, swallowed hard and continued. 'I was working in Melbourne when I got a phone call from my father saying I'd better get home ASAP. Something had happened to Marg, and she'd died.' He looked distraught.

The urge to tell him to stop rose again. He was hurting. She didn't want that. But she kept quiet. He had to do this his way.

He continued. 'The truth was that Marg committed suicide, and I never saw it coming. Nor did anyone close to her.'

Caia gasped. 'How did you cope? That must've been unbearable.' She shut up. No words could alter the pain he'd known. None that he wouldn't have heard time and again from people not knowing what to say.

'I didn't. I blamed myself for not realising something was wrong. The guilt was huge, and still rattles me at times. But I was also angry because she didn't talk to me, didn't say a word about wanting to take her own life, or why, or that she might've been depressed. Or anything.'

She reached for his hand, and held tight as they continued walking along the pathway.

Lockie remained quiet for a long while. Finally he stopped and turned to face her, dropping her hand as he did. 'Since then, I haven't trusted another woman enough to get close. Until you. Then I blew it because the fear of being hurt rose up fast when McKenzie called me daddy. She opened my eyes to what I was doing, and I suddenly thought I couldn't carry on, that I would only let you down if we got involved because I wasn't ready. Might never be.'

'But you're here telling me this.' It must've been hard. She always struggled talking about how her father and Garth had walked away from her. To talk about what his wife did was huge. Was he trying to tell her he cared for her and she could trust him? Or that she couldn't because he'd let his wife down? Nothing was straightforward anymore. 'Thank you, Lockie. I know it isn't easy.'

'The thing is, Caia, I finally woke up to the truth. I do want to be with you, to have a life with you. Since the day I met you at your interview, the sense of my dreams having a possibility of coming true has been growing to the point I can't deny it any longer. I've fallen in love with you, Caia.'

Caia stared at him as though she didn't know him. But then, she didn't really, because he hadn't been forthcoming about what made him tick. She'd obviously never expected him to tell her he loved her. Neither had he until this morning, when he knew he had to give this relationship all he had. And more. 'Caia?'

She stretched up to brush a kiss on his mouth, warming away the tension that'd been growing.

He returned her kiss before he set her back on her feet, keeping one arm around her shoulders. 'Tell me your story. Why did your father leave when you were so young? Why did McKenzie's father desert both of you?' He needed to know what held her back, because something did. It was there in the way she'd told him to leave her house last Saturday. Also how she trod around him on firm feet at work and not tiptoe. She protected herself first and foremost—after her daughter.

Her breasts rose and fell as she stared out across Auckland Harbour. When she finally spoke, it was quiet and unemotional. 'According to my grandmother, my father had no sense of responsibility, thought people should love him, not the other way round. Apparently he and my mother got on great until I came along. Then her attention was divided between him and me, and he hated that. One day he just packed his bags and left. From then on, Mum didn't have a lot of time for me either, being too engrossed in feeling sorry for herself.' Tension was rippling off her.

Lockie tightened his hold, bringing her closer to him. 'What about your grandmother? Did she keep an eye out for you?'

'She tried, but she wasn't well and died when I was about eight.'

'Sounds like you had a hard upbringing.'

'It was what it was.' Her shrug felt exaggerated, as though she didn't want to go into any more detail.

He understood, but after telling Caia about Marg, he knew talking had loosened the tightness he'd carried. 'What about McKenzie's father? You told me he left before she was born.'

'We were together eighteen months, and everything seemed rosy. Then I told him I was pregnant and he was gone, but not before he told me I'd let him down. He didn't want children, never had, and he wasn't changing his mind. He was gone unless I agreed to get rid of *it*. Something I'd never do. I had so much love waiting to be released, and my own child would never feel abandoned.'

'I'd have thought having a child in the relationship would make his case to get a Resident Visa stronger.'

'Apparently children come with too many demands and problems, and he didn't want to share his life with one.' Bitterness ricocheted off her tongue. 'Just like my father. Which is why I don't let men close anymore.'

That was a blow to his heart, but he'd take it. 'You're no slouch, Caia. You obviously learnt to be tough from early on.'

'I had to. I got my first job picking apples in an orchard near where we lived when I was twelve. I probably didn't do a great job, but the orchardist and his wife were so kind and kept encouraging me to do my best. I'd have picked twenty-four hours a day to please them. When I was a teenager, I doubt I'd have got through everything safely if not for them.' She slashed at her eyes. 'They were always there for me, and their daughter and I became best friends, almost sisters.'

'Izzy.'

She nodded. 'Izzy.'

'Where are her parents now?' Did they still support Caia as much as they used to? He wanted to meet them and thank them for helping her.

'They retired to the Gold Coast in Australia. Said it was time to relax and have some fun. But they turn up regularly to keep up with their granddaughters, including McKenzie.'

'They made you feel loved.'

Caia turned to stare up at him, the colour draining from her face. 'I don't always feel as if I am.'

He reached for her.

She stepped back. 'No, Lockie. How can I be when my father didn't want to know me? When Garth was using me for his own benefit?'

'How about when I love you and promise I'll never walk away from you? Can you accept I'm different? Believe that when I say I love you, it's true?' He couldn't say any more. His heart was beating so hard he thought it would crack apart.

Caia kept looking at him as the tension in her shoulders slowly relaxed. Slowly, slowly.

He waited, knowing if he opened his mouth again, she'd think he was trying too hard. He had no idea how long he waited, but suddenly she threw her arms around him and buried her face in his chest.

'I love you, too, Lockie. I do trust you. I want to be with you forever.'

His heart swelled. His head spun with happiness. He lifted her head with his fingers under her chin and leaned in to kiss this woman who meant the world to him. 'Forever it is.'

EPILOGUE

FIVE MONTHS LATER, sitting on the veranda at Lockie's home where Caia and McKenzie now lived, Caia held an envelope tight. 'The answer has arrived.' They'd been waiting impatiently for more than four weeks to learn whether or not Lockie was McKenzie's stem cell donor.

'Open the damned thing, will you?' Lockie grinned. 'I've waited too long already to wait another minute.'

The emerald on her engagement ring sparkled in the sun as she slid a finger under the seal. She was living the dream with Lockie. They got on so well she had to keep pinching herself to make sure it was real. Now they were about to find out the answer to the one question they'd had no answer for. 'It doesn't matter if you weren't the donor.'

'You know I won't be upset, but it would feel so right if I was. Another plus to our amazing little family.'

She knew he wasn't saying that he felt this would make him feel like McKenzie's dad, because already they'd seen a lawyer about Lockie becoming McKenzie's legal father. She had to admit it would be wonderful in a heartwarming way if Lockie had been the one to save McKenzie's life, adding to the fact he was a part of her life. Wait. She had something else to tell him. Before she opened the letter? Or after? 'Lockie, first I—'

'No first anything. Open that envelope. Please,' he added in the sexy voice he used when he was asking her to go down on him.

She grinned. 'You win.' She lifted the seal with her finger and snatched the letter out before Lockie beat her to it. After unfolding it, she scanned the page, looking for the answer.

'Caia, what are you doing to me?' Lockie leaned in and read the letter shaking in her hands. He lifted his head and locked his fierce gaze on her. 'Seriously? It *was* my bone marrow that McKenzie received?'

She nodded. 'So it says.' Why wouldn't they believe it? She read it again, slower this time to make sure she hadn't missed anything. 'You saved my girl.' Tears poured down her face, matching those covering Lockie's cheeks. Throwing her arms around him, she held on tight. 'You've saved me. You were always meant to be a part of our lives.'

'Mummy, Lockie, why are you crying?' McKenzie bounced impatiently on her little feet.

In one move, they pulled apart enough to wrap McKenzie into their hug. 'We're very happy, my girl.' Caia brushed a kiss on her daughter's forehead.

'Then why cry?'

'Sometimes people cry happy tears.'

Lockie looked at Caia with a question in his eyes.

'Go ahead.' It felt like the right moment for this.

'Remember the day you called me daddy, McKenzie?'

'Yes. You said you weren't.'

'Would you like to call me daddy again?'

'Yes, Daddy.' McKenzie leapt into the air before throwing her arms around him. 'I've got a daddy.'

'I've got more news,' Caia said softly.

Lockie looked at her. 'When is the baby due?'

There was no hiding anything from this man, and that made her happy. 'I'm eight weeks along.'

'After our wedding, then.'

'I'll need an expansive gown.' She giggled as he drew her in for another hug, this time gentle and loving and sublime. She couldn't ask for anything more.

'There's nothing more I want right now.' Lockie kissed her forehead. 'I love you all.'

* * * * *

If you enjoyed this story, check out these other great reads from Sue MacKay

Enemy on Her Hospital Ward
A Fling with the ER Doc
Parisian Surgeon's Secret Child
Wedding Date with the ER Doctor

All available now!